Ava

Halliday Family

Elizabeth Lennox

Table of Contents

Chapter 1

"I don't want his help!" Ava hissed, pacing across the lush courtyard filled with trees and flowering bushes.

And yet, she turned, pressing her hands against her eyes and forehead in a futile effort to find another solution. "There has to be another way!"

"Perhaps, if you asked nicely, I could offer an alternative."

The deep, harsh voice and clipped tones stopped her in her tracks. In fact, the sound stopped her heart. Before she spun around, Ava prayed that the familiar voice didn't belong to *him*! But when she turned, it was clear her prayers had been ignored.

"Grant!" Ava whispered, blue eyes wide as she took in the man's broad shoulders and towering height. Her two older brothers were several inches over six feet in height, but for some reason, Grant Hanover intimidated her in ways her brothers never had.

A dark eyebrow lifted as he gazed at her, hands tucked in the pockets of his immaculate, charcoal grey suit. "You're surprised to see me?" he asked, tilting his head slightly. "Did you fly twenty-three hundred miles to meet someone else?"

His features were rougher now, she suddenly realized. Better defined. His nose was sharper and it had clearly been broken at some point. His chin had been hidden under a rough beard when she'd last seen him, but he was clean shaven now. There had always been an aura of intensity, of power, about Grant. With an unexpected shiver, Ava noticed that it was still there, but it was tempered by...patience? Intelligence? Or perhaps it was merely the absolute conviction that he had the ability to crush anyone who dared to put an obstacle in his path?

Focus, she mentally admonished. Blinking, Ava smoothed a hand down over her outfit, even though she couldn't remember what she'd donned this morning. Lifting her chin, she tried to pretend a level of confidence she didn't feel.

"I came here to...," Ava swallowed hard, then abruptly stopped fidgeting. Staring into his uncompromising features, she wondered if she should admit anything now that she was face to face with him.

That ominous dark eyebrow lowered, but the sharply intelligent, green gaze narrowed. Something in his body language subtly shifted, but Ava couldn't quite define what had changed. However, his voice was gentler, gruff, but softer as he stated, "You came here to speak with me. To ask me for help."

Ava was startled by his calmly worded statement and almost stepped back. How in the world could he know that? Ava looked around, searching for the hidden cameras.

"They aren't there. I was arriving just as you walked into the building and I followed you here. I've been listening to you argue with the tree for the past five minutes."

Ava swallowed again, feeling more than a little foolish. "It's a nice tree," she replied, then barely restrained herself from rolling her eyes at herself.

"Is it?" he asked, looking up at the tree with sudden interest. It was a ficus and very leafy, but other than that, there wasn't anything special about it. "I'll mention to my gardener that he's doing a good job, then."

His teasing tone reminded her of...too many things. The memories came rushing back to her and she...Ava sighed heavily, her too-slender shoulders slumping. "This was a seriously bad idea," she muttered. "I'll head home now." She'd lost weight over the past few weeks. The stress of trying to resolve this problem, and not coming up with any possible solutions, defeated her.

Before she could reach the exit, his voice stopped her. "How is Pierce?" he asked, referring to Ava's oldest brother.

Confused, she turned back, tilting her head slightly. "Pierce?" she parroted, confused. She lifted a shoulder and shook her head slightly. "He's...fine, I guess."

Grant nodded slightly. There was an awkward pause. "He's still running Halliday Hotels?"

Ava nodded, crossing her arms over her stomach. "Yes. We're up to three hundred hotels and we're international now."

"That's good." He nodded slowly, as if that information was somehow profound. "Your family had just the one hotel outside of Seattle when we met, correct?"

Instantly, more of those memories flashed through her mind. The lake and the forests, the terror of those years after everyone left. One by one, the people in her life had left her. Her mother had died of cancer. Pierce had gone to Harvard. Felix...he'd joined the Navy. And Grant.

"Yes," she nodded, her body stiffening with the pain lashing at her from those memories. "Just the one. Originally."

More nodding, but this time, he added a slight uplift of one side of his mouth. "Impressive. Your brother had just returned from Harvard at the time, correct?"

She nodded again, gripping her elbows tightly. "Yes." She swallowed and, because he just kept standing there, his hands still shoved in his pockets, she added reluctantly, "That was the reason I couldn't go with you. Eight years ago." She squinted slightly as the sunshine suddenly slipped out from behind a cloud. "I had to help." When he didn't react, she continued but her tone sounded defensive now. "We were all struggling back then."

He nodded once more, a slow, almost disbelieving gesture. Had his lips tightened? Ava stared hard, but...he was such a mystery!

"Yes. I remember that's the excuse you gave me."

Instantaneous anger flared and she stepped forward, her hands dropping as her hands fisted by her sides. Ava wished she could poke him in the middle of his broad, muscular chest. But she wasn't brave enough to touch him, so she aimed for the air in front of him. Daring? No. However, Ava was painfully conscious of what used to happen whenever they touched years ago.

"It wasn't an 'excuse', Grant!" she snapped. "It was the truth!" She huffed a bit, then paced for two steps before coming back to glare up at him, needing to make Grant understand. "Pierce had just graduated. Jenna and I were barely making a profit at that small, roadside hotel when he came back and started helping with the business." And then, "I *couldn't* leave then!"

He didn't nod this time. He merely stared down at her. Ava had always hated the fact that she was the shortest in her family. But that fact was never so irritating as it was now. Not even her four inch, red heels helped. At five feet, four inches tall, her heels only brought her up to five-eight. Grant was still seven or eight inches taller than she was. Add in the broad muscular shoulders and lean hips, flat stomach and....

Ava remembered how stubborn...determined...Grant could be. She remembered that final argument and the desperation she'd felt when Grant hadn't understood. He'd never understood her. Not really. He'd come the closest to "getting" her. But in the end, he'd still left. Ava hadn't been enough for him and he'd walked away from her. From them!

Clearing her throat, she stepped back. "I'm sorry for wasting your time." She tried to step around him, but he was too big. Too broad. The dratted man took up too much space! She could either stomp on the flowers and possibly mess up her favorite red heels or she could stand here glaring at him!

She seriously considered stepping on the flowers, but before she could fully process that thought, he grabbed her upper arm and guided her towards the door.

"We'll talk," he snapped, yanking open the glass doors. He didn't lead her towards the bank of elevators. Instead, he pulled her towards a private elevator that pinged as soon as he pressed the button. They were inside and being lifted to the top floor before she thought to protest. Thankfully, he dropped her arm as soon as the elevator started moving, allowing Ava to step back.

"Nice to have a private lift," she grumbled, backing into a corner. But there wasn't enough space. Twenty-three hundred miles hadn't been enough space, she corrected. She'd dreamed about this man for eight years! A few extra feet in an elevator wasn't enough!

They'd both been staring up at the circles that lit up as the elevator rose through the floors. But at her grumbling comment, he turned his head, looking down at her with amused disbelief. "And you don't enjoy the luxuries your success allows?" he asked, lifting a dark eyebrow as he waited for her answer.

He had a point. The shoes she'd chosen for this meeting had cost over seven hundred dollars. They weren't even the most expensive in her wardrobe. They were just her favorites.

"You're right," she replied, but the anger in her tone diminished. "I apologize."

His eyes sparkled with amusement, although his lips remained stiff and resolute. "Old habits die hard, eh?"

The elevator doors opened, sparing her the need to respond. Not that she could, Ava thought and stepped out of the elevator, then waited for him to tell her which direction to go. He didn't tell her, he put a hand to the small of her back, guiding her down a long, luxuriously carpeted hallway. "Where are we going?" she asked, noticing the people in the offices along the way. Everyone seemed hard at work. But perhaps this was what it was like in the executive offices of Halliday Hotels. Pierce didn't allow slacking off. He worked extremely hard and expected his staff to work just as diligently. Apparently, Grant didn't allow idlers either.

Ava pushed herself to achieve the same measure of efficiency as the rest of her siblings, needing to prove to them that she could help, that her efforts were worthy of the outrageous amount of money she earned as part owner of Halliday Hotels.

The snick of the door closing behind her pulled her out of her thoughts again, reminding her that she needed to be aware of everything around Grant. He was insanely smart and knew how to take advantage of any show of weakness. It was one of the reasons he was disgustingly wealthy now.

"Have a seat," he ordered as he walked over to the bar. "What would you like to drink?"

"I'm fine," she replied flatly. She stood awkwardly in the middle of his office, wondering what to do with her hands. Several possibilities popped into her head, but she banished the erotic thoughts. She wasn't here to get back together with Grant. She'd come to...to...! To ask for help. But that had been a stupid impulse. She realized that now. So she was *not* going to ask!

Unaware of her mental machinations, Grant poured himself a portion of scotch and tossed it back in one gulp. She watched, fascinated, as he waited for the heat to hit him, then hissed as the smooth liquor warmed his chest. He glanced at her, and poured himself another before coming over to stand in front of her. "Stubborn as always, eh?" he asked.

Ava shuffled her feet uncomfortably. "I don't need to talk to you, Grant," she told him. "I've changed my mind." She stuffed her red leather clutch between her arm and her side, wishing she'd...what? Not come here? Not seen how incredibly handsome he still was?

No, that wasn't an accurate statement. Grant was even more attractive now than he'd been at twenty-five. Eight years had added depth to his character, smoothed out the rough edges. Money and power had added an additional layer of eye-catching complexity to his demeanor that couldn't be faked. He'd already been well on his way to success before. But now...now Grant was a terrifyingly powerful man!

And...goodness, he was *hot*!

Clearing her throat, she turned, suddenly desperate to leave. "I apologize for interrupting your day."

"What kind of help do you need?" he demanded. That stopped her progress, bringing back the previous tension.

She bowed her head, frustration and defeat tumbling around in her mind to create a bitter taste on her tongue.

Sometimes, life really sucked!

Slowly, she turned to face him again, but backed away several more steps, needing space to think. Despite her best efforts, Ava had to admit she was intimidated. "I don't require your help, Grant. I'll figure it out on my own."

His lips quirked at her declaration. "Obviously, you've gone through every scenario and already tried several ways to fix whatever is happening in your life. If you're here in Houston, prepared to ask me for help, then you're at rock bottom." He sat down on the sofa, spreading his arms wide along the back as he stretched his legs out in front of him. Ava watched, unable to pull her eyes away as he relaxed against the expensive leather. The man wasn't just hot, he was...well, outrageously sexy!

Ava turned her back to move over to the windows, looking out at the city below her. Houston was an enormous, high energy city. Grant had done extremely well for himself. She knew that he bought struggling businesses, fixed them, and then sold them for an outrageous profit. The business world trembled when he started looking into a company.

Yeah, she'd kept up with his success over the years. She'd tried to avoid looking for news of his success over the years. But Ava acknowledged a huge amount of pride in his success.

He wasn't just powerful. When Grant's attention turned to a company, investors knew it was in trouble. If he didn't take control of a floundering business, then the assumption was that it was too far gone and couldn't be saved. If he took control, the employees quaked in their boots. Because he always pruned the dead weight, changed things around, and pushed everyone to become more efficient and profitable.

He was an uncompromising and dangerous man.

Which was exactly why she'd come here to ask him for help. But seeing him again, she knew that this trip had been a mistake.

Grant clenched his teeth as Ava gazed out the window. In a way, her perusal of the city was a relief. Those stunning blue eyes of hers were no longer peering into his soul and, from this angle, he couldn't see her lush, perfect breasts and tiny waist, her slender hips and long legs. Had she worn those red heels because she remembered it was his favorite color?

She still had a great ass, he thought. His hands itched to cup that ass, to feel her squirm against him just like she used to all those years ago. Ava had been such an innocent when they first met. But he'd enticed her, taught her about her body, and shown her how to truly live. He'd helped her realize that she was a vibrant, amazing woman.

And then she'd discarded him like yesterday's trash.

So, what the hell was going on that was bad enough to bring her here?

"How is your sister?" he asked, breaking the silence.

She spun around, not quite making eye contact. He noticed how long and dark her eyelashes were. Hell!

She kept her arms locked, ostensibly to keep her purse securely tucked against her body. But he knew Ava. Her body language was all protectiveness.

"She's fine. Jenna is still...perfect."

Grant easily recalled the tension between the sisters. Ava hadn't ever felt like she could live up to Jenna's standards, but Grant knew Ava had made a significant contribution to the success of their hotels. Did Ava realize how much her designs were talked about within the industry? Probably not.

"And your other brother?"

Had she relaxed slightly? "Felix?"

Grant tilted his head slightly. "He survived the Navy then? Eight years ago, you were so certain that he was going to end up dead after he was selected into the Special Forces."

She shrugged, one finger tapping nervously against her arm, but the pride was clear in her tone when she talked about her second oldest brother. "He was a good SEAL. He spent several years doing...things... around the world. And yes, he's back. He's in charge of building the new hotels and renovating the new acquisitions."

"I thought Pierce bought up previously established hotels and converted them to the Halliday methods."

The finger stopped tapping and she smile faintly. "He does. But we also build when there isn't a hotel in a specific market." She smiled more broadly now, thinking of her brothers. "Pierce excels at finding cities that need additional hotel space."

Grant nodded, watching her carefully. His protective instincts were screaming right now. Something was seriously wrong in her world. But if Ava needed a bit of conversation to help her relax, then he'd chat. "So I've read. He's quite the terror in the hospitality industry."

She laughed and the sound not only brightened his soul, it lightened her features, turning her from stunning to achingly beautiful. "That sounds a bit contradictory, don't you think?"

He frowned uncomprehendingly and she explained. "Terror and hospitality don't exactly go hand in hand."

Grant chuckled at her statement, then shrugged slightly. "They do when referring to your brother. I've invested a great deal of money in Halliday Hotels. He's incredibly good." He sighed and sipped his drink. "So, Pierce gobbles up ailing hotels and Felix builds new ones. What does Jenna do?"

Ava tensed at the mention of her older sister. Pierce was the oldest at about thirty-five now, then Felix who was two years younger. Grant knew that Ava never felt as if she measured up to Jenna who was only two years older than Ava. As the youngest of the Halliday clan, Grant remembered that Ava had always struggled to keep up with her more ambitious siblings.

"Jenna runs the hotels. Pierce deals with the larger issues, such as expansion and finances, while Jenna manages the day to day operations." She sighed and looked away. "She's brilliant, actually. The staff worship her because she's fair and generous. Halliday Hotels pays better than any other hotel chain in the industry and we have very generous benefits. That breeds loyalty, and that has helped us enormously with our success over the years. Jenna...is amazing."

"That's good. A loyal staff works harder and better than a staff that hates their job."

She smiled, but her features were stiff. "Exactly." She nodded towards the glass in his hand. "I think I will have that drink after all, if you don't mind."

Grant watched her, surprised but almost relieved. He stood up and hesitated. She looked on the edge of...something. Her request for a drink was another clue. In his memory, Ava had never been a drinker. She would occasionally drink a root beer when she felt wild. Never alcohol.

She'd definitely changed over the years.

When she lifted a sleek eyebrow at his hesitation, he almost chuckled. Impudent woman! However, he moved to the bar, setting his glass down as he took another and poured a generous amount of scotch. When he handed it to her, Grant noticed that she went out of her way to avoid touching his fingers. Interesting.

He paused before heading back to the sofa, watching her take a tentative sip, and chuckled when she coughed.

"How about a glass of wine instead?" he offered, trying, and failing, to hide his amusement.

She smiled slightly, but the expression faded quickly away. "No, this is fine," she insisted, still clutching her red purse between her arm and body, but now she also protected the glass, pressing it against her chest.

Lucky glass, he thought as he returned to the sofa.

Sitting down, he continued to watch her. She sipped the scotch as she worked through some issue in her mind. Hopefully, the alcohol would help calm her a little. The woman was stretched tighter than a bowstring!

"So, what do you do for the hotel?" he asked, wanting to hear her voice even though he knew the answer. He was such a glutton for punishment! Even the sound of her voice turned him on. It had always been like that. From the first moment he'd met her, he'd loved listening to her talk. Her voice was soft and lilting, her eyes glowing with excitement or darkening when something was wrong. And when he'd kissed her, she'd gasp with delight as his hands stroked her skin. She'd been a joy to make love to because...!

Shifting, he hid his body's reaction to those memories. Not the time, he reminded himself firmly. It would most likely never be the time again. Damn it!

"I decorate."

Grant noticed she didn't elaborate and her features looked...tight. Almost as if she resented her role within the Halliday organization. That resentment confused him. Eight years ago, Ava had loved decorating, styling the various rooms so that they were more interesting, more intriguing for the guests. She loved taking pictures of each of her designs, getting just the right angle and featuring the best aspects of her designs in those photos.

Coming up with a new idea, a new theme, had energized her back then.

So he asked, "Do you enjoy it?"

She grimaced and turned away. But the stiffness in her shoulders warned him that Ava was angry about something.

"I'm also in charge of marketing. And yes, I enjoy both. The artistic, creative side of the business appeals to me."

"Marketing is highly important to any business."

He saw her sigh as her shoulders fell. "I used to do all of the marketing myself. It was fun and easy. But as our business grew, Jenna suggested that I focus more on the décor aspect and we hired someone else to handle the marketing. She left the marketing staff under my prevue though. So I'm still technically in charge of marketing."

"Would you prefer to do the marketing? Or the décor?"

She shrugged and turned around, her eyes angry. "They gave me the easy stuff," she snapped. "They don't want me to be involved in the day to day operations, so they slowly shifted me to decorating."

He was surprised by her anger and didn't completely understand it. "From what I've read, Halliday Hotels are renowned for their décor. Every time your family opens a new hotel, or after you take over a hotel, there's a buzz of anticipation to see the décor." He leaned forward, bracing his elbows on his knees as he took another sip of the scotch. "I would say that the décor is the main allure of the Halliday Hotels. It's strong and vibrant, a vital part of the reason that the hotels stand out in a guest's mind."

She smiled slightly, but the expression quickly disappeared. "Thank you for that."

Her response bothered him because he wasn't sure what she was thanking him for. Was she grateful for the assessment of her skills or because he'd given her a compliment?

Abruptly, he stood up. "I'm hungry. How about Italian for dinner?" He drained the remaining scotch in his glass and set it on the coffee table.

Ava stiffened suddenly, shaking her head and taking a small step backwards. "I don't...we aren't...!"

"Nonsense," he interrupted, taking her barely touched glass of scotch and putting it on the bar. "You're hungry and I doubt that you've changed so much that you don't still love pasta with lots of cheese."

He put a hand to the small of her back and led her out of his office, determined to feed her now that he'd noticed he could feel her ribs. She was too thin, he thought in dismay. Damn it, why did he care? She was here to ask a favor of him. Not because she wanted to get back in bed with him. Not that he would, Grant reminded himself. He'd done just fine without Ava all these years. His business was bigger and more profitable than even he'd imagined eight years ago. He'd lived and breathed business, spending twenty or more hours a day finding and fixing businesses, then finding just the right buyer to take over and pay him a tidy profit for his efforts.

It wouldn't hurt to take a few hours off so that he could feed a woman who was obviously in need of help. Even if it was just a good meal, he was determined to do what he could to help Ava. He didn't know exactly why that determination was so strong, but he couldn't ignore his protective instincts. Something was seriously wrong in Ava's life and she needed help.

Chapter 2

Ava eyed the enormous plate of pasta in front of her. With a sigh, she picked up her glass of wine and took a long sip, closing her eyes to better appreciate the flavors. The wine was delicious, smooth with fruity accents, and a delicious creamy aftertaste. She'd never learned to drink scotch and bourbon the way her brothers and Jenna did, but wine? Oh yes, she loved wine. A great pair of shoes to power through the day and an excellent glass of wine at the end to enjoy were two of the luxuries she allowed herself.

"Where did you get that dress?" he asked, interrupting her sensual appreciation for the wine.

Ava's eyes popped open and she frowned quizzically at Grant across the table. "Dress?"

She glanced down at her outfit, smoothing a hand over the soft wool. It was a red dress with pink slashes going in different angles. The dress hugged her figure and made her feel powerful and daring! The reality of her life was the complete opposite, hence her presence here in Houston, searching for help.

"Yes. The dress is interesting. I like the cut of it."

"Oh. Um...." She carefully set her wine glass down on the linen covered table with a precision that seemed a little odd. "Well, the dress is from a small boutique in Seattle," she lied. Ava peeked through her lashes at Grant to see if he believed her. Nope! The suspicious glint in his eyes warned her that he could still tell when she lied. Time for a bit of distraction, she thought. And maybe she could get enough information from him to solve her problem on her own. Oh, wouldn't that be wonderful! Her siblings wouldn't need to know how badly she'd messed up and she could finish what she'd started!

"You have an old friend by the name of Willy Zanika, right?"

Immediately, his body tensed. It wasn't so much as a stiffening, but more like the air around Grant began to crackle with energy. How he did that, she wasn't sure, but it was an interesting trick.

"No."

Ava blinked, confused by his response. "No, you don't know Mr. Zanika?" she asked, needing clarification.

"I know him, but we are definitely not friends." He leaned forward and that crackling energy moved with him, seeming to dance over her skin, leaving tingles in its wake. "Stay away from Willy, Ava. He's dangerous."

Oh, didn't she know that firsthand! "Yes, but...what do you know of him?" she probed. She picked up her fork, not because she was hungry, but because she needed to do something with her hands, something that would make her question appear more casual than it was.

"Why do you want to know?"

She shrugged, twirling spaghetti around her fork. "Just a casual question, Grant," she lifted the fork to her mouth. "If you don't know Willy, then just say so."

She took a bite of her food and...Oh, this pasta was delicious! It was fresh pasta in a red sauce with basil and garlic, but there were undertones to the sauce that were absolutely perfect!

Grant pulled her attention away from the food. "Willy Zanika is a bastard. He's a low level thug that likes to hurt people." Grant leaned forward slightly, watching her intently. "Ava, if he's doing something, if he's threatened you, then I need to know."

She took another long sip of her wine, which paired perfectly with the red sauce. "No worries," she replied in a blasé tone. Goodness, the wine was excellent! "I wonder who the chef is here. This red sauce is amazing!" She took another bite, then carefully blotted her mouth with the linen napkin. "I'll have to mention this place to Jenna. She's always looking for good chefs." Ava tilted her head slightly as if considering something. "I don't understand why though. It would seem that one chef and a bunch of line cooks would be enough. But apparently, there are several layers of chefs within a professional kitchen." She leaned forward, her eyes sparkling. "Did you know that? Did you know that there are executive chefs, *sous* chefs, *sommis* chefs, and a few others that," she waved a hand breezily, "...I have no idea what they do, but I definitely enjoy watching them do their thing." She giggled, then covered her mouth. "And another mystery...I don't understand how they can cut things so quickly without losing a finger!"

Goodness, it was warm in this restaurant. She took another bite of the excellent pasta, sighing happily as the carbs and the wine soothed the

tension that seemed to be ever-present in her life lately.
"Do you not like your pasta?' she asked, glancing down at his risotto with seafood.
"It's fine," he replied, completely ignoring his meal. "How about more wine?"
"Ooh! That would be lovely!" she replied, unaware of how she wiggled her butt against the seat in anticipation.

Grant watched as Ava took another long sip of the wine. She'd barely finished the first glass of wine and, apparently, she was still a lightweight when it came to alcohol. He only poured her half a glass this time. He didn't want her drunk, but she was definitely more relaxed now.
"How do you know Willy?"
"I don't," she replied quickly enough that he was confident that she was telling the truth.
"So, why do you want to know about him?"
She twirled more pasta on her fork. "Because he's a horrible person and I don't want him messing things up for me."
A bolt of icy terror hit him. "How is he messing things up for you?"
She laughed and took another bite of pasta. "He's not."
"He's not?"
She laughed, chewing the pasta as she sighed with pleasure. "Goodness, it's been a while since I've had pasta."
"Why?"
She glanced at him over the rim of her wine glass. "Why what?"
Grant was alternately amused and frustrated by her inability to focus on the conversation. "Why has it been so long since you've eaten pasta? I thought you loved pasta."
"I did." She laughed, covering her mouth as if she'd done something wrong. "I do." She looked down at her plate, then giggled again. "Obviously, I still love pasta. Especially when there is a tasty sauce on it." Her brows furrowed. "But there isn't enough cheese on this pasta. I *really* love cheese." Grant was about to beckon a waiter over so that he could request more cheese. But her next words stopped him. "Cheese is really bad though. It's not healthy and I'm trying to be healthier." She lifted her eyes and he noticed that they were glazed over, either from the carbs or the wine, he wasn't sure which. Most likely the wine, but he didn't discount the effects of pasta.
"What are you doing to be healthier?"
She sipped her wine and smiled, leaning back in the upholstered chair, cradling the wineglass against her chest. Again, he felt a surge of jeal-

ousy for an inanimate object.

"Well, a few years ago, I started running. I enjoy the challenge of going just a little further every day." She grinned. "I ran a half marathon several months ago and I registered to run another one in the fall."

"Excellent!" Grant replied, truly impressed. "I didn't think that you liked running."

"I didn't." She waved her hand in the air. "At least, when I was younger, I didn't know how to run." She squinched up her nose. "I *hated* running in high school," she started, emphasizing "hated" as if it were venom. "First of all, all the other students were in better shape and would make fun of me because I was such a slow runner. But the phys-ed teachers never really taught us *how* to run." She sighed and took another sip of wine, then continued. "The teachers would just tell us all to start running, then click their evil stop-watch to time all the students." She made a sound that he would have sworn was a growl, but this was Ava. She was so delicate, he couldn't imagine her ever making such an amusing sound, and so he discounted what he had heard. "There's a technique to it, you know. It's not just 'do it'. There are breathing techniques, pacing, the way one holds their hands, and foot placement. Running is a fascinating science."

He was an avid runner himself. He'd started running right after leaving Seattle, actually. He'd used running and weight lifting as a way to banish Ava from his thoughts.

Although, it hadn't worked. Nothing had worked.

And now, here they were.

"I think I'm drunk, Grant!" she said in a stage whisper.

He looked over at her, stunned as he realized that, yes, Ava was definitely leaning slightly to the side. She'd had only a glass and a half of wine and she was drunk? Damn, that was...unexpected. He'd thought to get her a bit tipsy so that she would tell him about the problem that had brought her here to Houston. Now what was he going to do?

Her eyes were drifting closed. She was half asleep already!

"Ava!" he snapped.

She jerked awake, gazed across the table at him, and smiled. "You've gotten more handsome over the years." She sighed, and smiled goofily. "And I never forgot you." She lifted a finger. "I probably shouldn't tell you this, but I still dream about you!"

He was stunned. Dreams? She dreamt about him? Or them, together?

"What kind of dreams?" he asked, lifting his hand to signal the waiter. The bill was brought immediately and Grant tossed some money on top of it, enough for the bill and a large tip. Then he came around and helped Ava to her feet. She had to lean heavily against him, but she was still able to walk, thank goodness. He didn't think there were any reporters in the restaurant, but it wouldn't be good if they were recognized. He could just see the headlines; 'Tycoon gets Famous Designer Drunk'. No, he doubted Ava would appreciate that. So he wrapped his arm around her, ignoring the fact that she still fit against his side perfectly, and nearly carried her out of the restaurant. Thankfully, his driver was waiting, probably alerted by the restaurant staff.

"Where to, sir?" his driver asked, once they were settled in the backseat.

Grant looked down at Ava. She was sound asleep, leaning against his shoulder. No way would she remember which hotel she was staying at. It was most likely one of her family's hotels. There were three in Houston. But perhaps she hadn't registered at a family hotel, not wanting her visit here to get back to her siblings.

There was only one thing he could do. "Home. She'll stay with me tonight."

Chapter 3

Ava woke up with a start and looked wildly around, then grabbed the sheet to cover her nakedness. Well, she wasn't completely naked, she realized. She still wore her bra and panties. Where was her dress? And her shoes? Yes, she definitely wanted to locate her shoes.

"Not good!" she whispered.

Looking out the window, she noticed that the sun was just starting to come up over the horizon. "Okay, so it's morning." Or night? Was it still night? Or the next night? How long had she slept?

The wine! She'd gotten drunk last night! "Darn it!" she whispered, pushing her hair out of her face. "No more wine!" Or at least, no more than half a glass, which was her normal limit.

Scraps of memories of the night before came back to her. "Grant!" she hissed, putting a hand to her aching head. "What have I done?"

Pasta. Good pasta! And excellent wine. Too much wine. Why had she drunk that second glass? She knew that she had no tolerance for wine! Especially good wine!

"I need to get out of here."

Before she could move, a knock sounded on the door. She pulled the sheet up higher, then called out, "Come in?"

An impossibly handsome Grant stepped into the room carrying two steaming mugs of coffee. "Good. You're awake," he said, bringing her a mug. He was wearing clothes, but barely. The jeans he'd pulled on rode low on his lean hips and his shirt was left open. He hadn't shaved yet and he looked...even better than last night's pasta.

"Coffee?" he asked, offering her a mug.

"Yes. Thank you." Ava accepted the coffee, but struggled to keep the sheet up over herself at the same time. Finally, she had the cup and the sheet secured, and was grateful when Grant backed up slightly. "I'm sorry about last night. I didn't mean to get drunk."

He chuckled, took a sip of his coffee, and leaned back against the dresser in what she assumed was the guest bedroom.

"So, are you going to tell me why you flew all the way out here to Houston to speak with me?"

Ava sipped her coffee, waiting for the rush of caffeine to hit her, then sighed. "No."

He laughed softly, shaking his head.

She couldn't hide her defensiveness when she added, "And I'm especially not going to tell you anything when I'm lying in a strange bed with no clothes on." She nodded towards the door. "If you wouldn't mind, I'd like to get dressed."

He tilted his head to the side in acknowledgement. "Fair enough. I had some new clothes delivered for you." He pushed away from the dresser and moved to the doorway. He picked up a bag from one of Houston's designer boutiques and set it on the end of the bed. "The shower is through that door and...," his gaze dropped to the strap of her black bra, "...well, I'll wait for you in the kitchen."

Ava waited until the door closed behind him before she took another sip of coffee, wishing she had some pain relievers for her headache. "A hangover is what you deserve," she whispered, climbing out of bed with a sigh. Still cradling the coffee, she grabbed the bag and hurried into the bathroom, worried that Grant might return.

After a shower and slipping into the new clothes, soft leggings and an oversized sweatshirt with pretty panties and bra, she felt much better. He hadn't gotten her any makeup, but that was okay. She didn't wear a lot anyway.

Piling her hair up on top of her head, she grabbed her now-empty coffee cup and padded barefoot out to the kitchen. Grant's home was huge, and the kitchen filled with light and lots of counterspace.

"I bet your housekeeper loves cooking in here," she whispered, jealous of the wide expanse of the island. Ava loved to bake, and making bread was one of her favorite ways to relax. There was nothing as good as kneading bread to work out the stress from a long meeting.

"My housekeeper comes in to clean and do laundry. I do the cooking," he announced, moving over to the oven to bring out a plate stacked high with pancakes. "I hope you're hungry."

"Pancakes?" she whispered as she stared hungrily at the stack. "I haven't had pancakes since..." she stopped, memories of that last time washing over her. It had been with him. Their last morning together. He'd made her pancakes, then...well, she didn't think about that morning often.

"Dig in," he urged. He came around to the other side of the island and sat down next to her. He'd already set out plates and utensils, as well as butter and syrup. "So why are you here? What's going on that you need help with?"

She sighed, taking two pancakes, then adding a pat of butter to each.

"I just wanted information about Willy Zanika," she explained, pouring the maple syrup over her pancakes. By now, her mouth was watering. "What can you tell me about him and his business?"

"He doesn't have a business," Grant told her, pouring maple syrup on his pancakes. "He has criminal enterprises. From what I gathered from his past efforts, he's into racketeering, extortion, and probably worse."

"Worse?" she asked, her voice cracking in alarm. She stared at his handsome, but serious, features as the bite of pancake turned to a rock in her stomach.

"I know that the FBI is looking at him for human trafficking."

Those two words were enough to send terror through any woman's heart. "That's horrible!"

"Exactly. So, stay away from him." He looked down at her, his eyes assessing her pale features. "But, it's too late, isn't it?"

Ava sighed, her shoulders slumping. All of a sudden, her appetite was gone. "It's okay," she lied. "I can handle him."

Grant put his knife and fork down and turned to face her. "Ava, there's no 'handling' Willy. He's a criminal of the worst kind. He is a very smart man and could probably be a great businessman if he were ever willing to put his intelligence to legal methods of making money. But he prefers the illegal aspect of his efforts. He enjoys terrorizing people." He paused, ensuring that she was paying attention before he said, "And he loves hurting them."

She cringed and, for a brief moment, she let the terror inside of her show on her face. But she looked quickly away, trying to hide her reaction.

"That's good to know." She wiped her mouth with the linen napkin, setting it carefully beside her barely touched pancakes. "I'll stay far away from him. Thank you for the information."

She stood up, grabbed her purse, and looked around. "I should be on my way. I'll call a cab to the airport."

Grant shook his head. "I'm not letting you leave without knowing exactly what's going on with Willy."

Ava tilted her head slightly. "Why do you use his first name?"

"Because he and I used to be friends. That was before I knew what he was like underneath the façade of civility. I *almost* went into business with him."

"Why didn't you?'

He shrugged and he noticed her gaze dropped briefly to his shoulders before returning to his face. Grant remembered her gripping his shoulders, her nails digging into his muscles when he brought her to a climax.

Pushing the memory aside, he forced himself to focus on the current situation. "Willy and I stopped being friends the day I saw his true nature. He doesn't bother me now."

"How..." Ava stopped when her voice cracked from the strain. She cleared her throat and tried again. "How did you get him to stop bothering you?"

"I have...something...that Willy doesn't want the public to see."

"What's that?"

Grant hesitated, not wanting Ava to get in the middle of a battle that had been raging for several years. "It's not important. I just need to know that you won't get involved with Willy."

She lifted a hand as if she were giving an oath. "I swear, I will avoid him like the plague!"

Chapter 4

"What in the world?!" Ava gasped, her eyes latching onto the familiar figure walking confidently across the hotel lobby. Her hotel! Well...her family's hotel.

Grant was here? In Seattle?! Why in the world was he here? She'd left him back in Houston with a smile and a solemn agreement to avoid Willy Zanika.

So, why was he here?

Before she could breathe, the man in question hesitated, turning to look directly into her stunned, horrified eyes.

He was here! He was in her "home", so to speak.

Immediately, he changed direction, coming straight for her. Ava broke eye contact and looked around, not sure what to do. Should she hide? No, he'd already seen her. Should she confront him? Maybe she could act like they were just friends?

Yes, that's what she would do. Clutching her leather bound notebook to her chest, as if it could shield her from the intense potency of his presence, she forced her lips into a smile. Ava was just about to utter a polite greeting when he ripped the notebook out of her hands and pulled her into his arms.

Within moments, she was clinging to him, her mind blank as his kiss echoed through her body. He pulled her closer as the power of his touch, his kiss, caused her knees to wobble.

Ava hadn't meant to kiss him back! She shouldn't be kissing him! Nor should she moan and press closer, aligning her curves so they fit more perfectly against the hardness of his body.

In the background, she vaguely heard someone whimper, but Ava was too caught up in reacquainting herself with the deliciousness of Grant's mouth and all of those yummy muscles that rippled under her fingers as she moved her hands down over his shoulders, then his arms. Oh my, the man knew how to kiss!

When he straightened, someone whimpered again. She didn't like that noise. It sounded...desperate and she wished that whoever it was would stop.

"Good morning," he grumbled, low and sexy. He sounded like he'd just made love to her. Or maybe he sounded like they'd just woken up and she'd rolled over into his arms. He sounded as if he were about to make love to her again!

No, correction. That had been the dream she'd woken from this morning. Several hours ago, Ava had been alone in her bed trying to blink away memories of the wildly erotic dream. Hours ago, she'd been alone and aching to feel him touch her exactly like this.

But "this" was real! Not a dream. And "this" was bad! She and Grant weren't a couple. Not anymore! They hadn't been a couple for eight, long, painful years! So, why had she kissed him back? She'd kissed Grant like he was her long, lost lover.

Correction, she'd kissed him as if they were currently lovers.

Oh, this was *so* not good.

"What are you doing here?" she whispered. Then she suddenly remembered where "here" was and pulled away, looking around nervously. Hopefully, none of the staff, or worse, her siblings, had seen her kissing Grant in the middle of the lobby. Personal displays of affection were perfectly fine, perhaps even encouraged to some degree, in the hotel lobbies. But not PDAs involving the hotel owners! And as a major shareholder in Halliday Hotels, Ava was definitely considered an "owner" and should display better decorum.

"You're in trouble with a very bad man," he murmured.

Ava ignored the sinking sensation in her heart. Okay, so maybe she'd hoped he'd say something along the lines of, "After I saw you in Houston, I couldn't stop thinking about you and remembering how much you meant to me."

She narrowed her eyes. "And you came here to what? Be my white knight?"

He chuckled, then pulled her against his side, and returned her leather notebook. "Something like that."

She gripped the notebook, and started walking, not sure exactly where they were going.

"Seriously Grant, why are you here?"

"Because you're in trouble, Ava," he replied firmly. "And I'm probably the only person who can keep Willy from hurting you."

She swallowed hard as unexpected warmth began bubbling in her stomach. This was ridiculous. He just showed up and her emotions went on a wild roller coaster ride? Absolutely ridiculous!

"Where are you leading me now?" she demanded, suddenly realizing that they were walking together.

"We're going to have lunch. During the meal, you're going to explain all of the reasons you're not willing to ask your brother for help."

She bit her lip as she waited for him to pull the door open for her. She paused before walking through it. "How do you know I didn't already go to Pierce?"

"Because you never would have shown up in Houston if Pierce had been an option." He glanced down at her as they came to a halt in front of a chauffeured limousine. "You might have rejected me eight years ago, Ava. But I suspect that you haven't changed all that much since then, have you?"

There was a lot to unpack in that statement and she stared up at him, not sure if she should be angry about him knowing how she felt about her oldest brother, or the fact that he claimed she broke up with him.

"I can see the fury building up in your eyes, Ava," he chuckled, his voice doing that sexy thing again, sending shivers down her spine. "But how about if we have this argument in the privacy of the limousine instead of out here on the sidewalk where others might hear us and start recording on their cell phones?"

He was right, damn it! Ava glanced around, noticed the curious stares of the people on the sidewalk. Instead of snapping at him again, she ducked into the back of the vehicle, wishing he was...well, anywhere but here! Some might say she wanted him dead, but Ava didn't want that. She couldn't imagine a world in which Grant wasn't alive and well. She might hate him, but she didn't want anything bad to happen to him.

Grant ducked into the limousine after her and she quickly scooted over to make room for him. After that kiss in the lobby, Ava suspected she shouldn't get too close to him. Obviously, he still had the power to turn her into mush, even after all these years.

He settled in the leather seat beside her and the driver pulled away from the curb. Grant pressed a button, closing the window between them and the driver, ensuring their privacy. "Okay, so explain what's *really* going on."

"Nothing," she said firmly, crossing her arms over her chest. She noticed she didn't even have her purse. She had her cell phone, because she'd learned never to go anywhere without her cell phone. It was her lifeline and the few times she'd found herself without it, she'd panicked.

He chuckled and she hated how much she enjoyed the sound.

"I'll tell you what," he started again, shifting slightly to look at her more fully. "I have a series of business dinners lined up over the next week or so. I need a date, someone who can converse intelligently during the meals."

"You need a barbie doll?" she snapped, her heart twisting painfully at the idea of Grant with another woman.

"No," he stated firmly. "I need an intelligent woman who doesn't make inane comments or check her makeup every five minutes. I need someone smart, someone knowledgeable about a wide range of subjects."

She rolled her eyes, huffing impatiently as she twisted so she was staring straight ahead. "While you and the big boys work on complicated business deals that us little girls can't possibly understand?" she challenged.

"Business discussions will be conducted during business hours. You work on your business issues during business hours as well. But in the evening, you will join me for dinners where we will be seen together. That will help keep the other women away, but you being with me will also show Willy that you are under my protection. He won't hurt you or threaten you as long as he thinks we are together."

Startled, Ava blinked at him. She tried to hide the hopeful pounding of her heart, but suspected that Grant saw and knew everything. "Why?" she asked.

"Like I said, I have information that he doesn't want out in the open. And I want to protect you."

Ava ignored the warmth that seeped into her heart at his words. "Okay but...why?"

He laughed leaning back against the seat. "Because you need me." He glanced at her. "And you're going to explain why you need my protection."

"I am?"

"Absolutely. Over lunch, you'll explain and I'll be able to better protect you against the obnoxious Willys of this world. In return, you'll protect me from avaricious women who see me as their meal ticket. It's a win-win situation."

Ava stared at him for a long moment. Finally, she broke the silence to ask, "Why me? You could hire someone to sit with you during business dinners and not have to sully your hands with the criminal element."

He shrugged as if the answer weren't very important. "You're free," he countered.

She snorted. "You are disgustingly wealthy and could afford a hired escort."

"Said the kettle," he countered, referring to the kettle and the pot both being black.

"I'm not in the same realm you are, Grant. I have money but–"

"Halliday Hotels and your other investments have made you into one of the wealthiest women in the country, Ava."

She snorted, waving a hand dismissively. "So, you just need someone to show up on your arm and I need someone to..." she stopped abruptly, biting her lip.

"What's going on, Ava?"

Ava didn't answer immediately. Did she have any other options? No, not really. She could go to Pierce and he would probably know how to fix this mess. Or she could go to Felix. His training as a Navy SEAL could fix the problem pretty easily. But Ava suspected that Felix would simply hunt the bastard down and...well, no one would ever find the body. Felix was *that* scary. Besides, he was the one who designed and built the hotels. Willy might end up buried underneath several thousand tons of concrete. And Felix might eventually be arrested for murder.

No, Felix simply wasn't an option. He was a warrior. Always had been.

Jenna?

Ava almost choked at the thought of bringing this to Jenna. Her older sister by two years would most likely...what would Jenna do? Ava had no idea how Jenna got things done. Every problem was dealt with, every issue was just...magically fixed. The woman was a miracle worker.

However, Ava couldn't involve Jenna in this mess. This was her problem. Ava had to solve it herself.

"Fine," she snapped and turned to frown at Grant.

"Does this have anything to do with the art exhibit you're organizing?"

She gasped. "How did you hear about the art exhibit?"

"I know things, Ava. Information has always been more powerful than money. You should know that by now."

She slumped back against the seat, nibbling at her lower lip, trying to decide how much to tell him.

"All of it," he asserted firmly.

Ava glared at him. But she sighed and started explaining. "It took me almost five months to convince Pierce," she paused and peeked up at him through her eyelashes.

"What did you convince him to do?" he prompted.

She thought back to the night her oldest brother had left for college. She'd been devastated. But not nearly as devastated as when...well, that was in the past, she told herself firmly. Taking a deep breath, she continued her story. "Pierce went off to Harvard. Felix had just joined the Navy." She paused, thinking back to those terrifying days. "All those years ago, Jenna and I were left to run the hotel by ourselves."

"Only you and Jenna? Where was your father?"

Her father. Goodness, her father. "He was around. Just..." She waved a hand expressively.

"Not sober," he supplied. The silence was heavy for a long moment.

"Correct. My father was...well, he was a drunk." She wasn't going to sugar coat her family history. Not anymore. "He was always around, but never much help. In fact, he was pretty much always a hindrance. Anytime we made..." she stopped again. "Irrelevant to this situation."

"And you're not going to tell me what happened to your father?"

She shrugged, glancing out the window again. "Like I said, he's not relevant to the story now." She took a deep breath, then continued. "As I was saying, it took me a while to convince Pierce to allow me to do this art exhibit in the Seattle hotel's lobby and ballroom. It took a while, but I managed to line up several promising, local artists. They are all eager for the show and the potential exposure." She gritted her teeth for a long moment, wondering what she could have done differently to avoid this situation. "Somehow, Mr. Zanika heard about the exhibit. He approached me while I was eating lunch one day."

"What restaurant?"

"Does it matter? It was my office."

He thought about it for a moment and shook his head. "I suppose not."

She sighed and stared blindly out the window. She didn't see the trees passing by. It was summer now. Just like eight years ago.

Pushing the memories aside, she focused on the present. "Mr. Zanika barged into my office one day, closed the door so my assistant couldn't hear our conversation. He then proceeded to explain that he would set the prices for each of the art pieces. He would manage the exchange of money through his credit card system and the artists would be happy with whatever portion of the price he deigned to give them." She blinked back the tears. "He said the exhibit would be the perfect way for him to launder a bit of the cash he had lying around." She pressed her lips together for a moment. "He said that I should arrange more art exhibits in the future and at the other hotels around the country, because he anticipated that this would be an excellent way for him to get clean cash, but he also wants me to introduce him to the various buyers." She sighed heavily, looking up at Grant. "He's going to use those introductions for bad things, isn't he?"

Grant nodded grimly. "Yes. He is."

"That's what I thought. So not only are the artists only going to get a fraction of the price for their art pieces, Mr. Zanika is going to manipulate their potential clients." She took a deep breath, not wanting to show Grant just how upset she was by the mess she'd created.

"He's not going to do anything to you or your clients. He's going to stay far away from the hotel, you, the artists, and everyone's clients."

She stared up at him, comforted by the finality in his voice. "How do you know? Why won't you tell me what you have on him?"

He looked at her through hooded eyes for a long moment, then said, "You're safer if you don't know."

She didn't like the sound of that. "Will this put you in danger?"

"No."

That succinct reply somehow made her feel significantly better. His confidence was...contagious? No, that wasn't the right word. But as she looked at him, saw the determination and confidence in his eyes, she felt a wave of relief so intense that it made her slightly giddy. "Thank you."

"Don't thank me yet. You will have to do a lot to convince Willy that you're under my protection."

Why were his eyes burning now? Was there some secret she should know about? What was his relationship with Willy Zanika? How had a businessman and a criminal met?

The possibilities sent a chill down her spine.

"Where are we going?" she asked. "I have work to do."

He lifted his phone and pressed a button. "Head back to the Halliday Hotel, Jim," he said into the phone. She assumed he'd spoken to the driver because the limousine took an immediate right and they were heading back into the city. All of the executive offices were located right next to the Seattle hotel location.

"Why are your offices located so close to one of your hotels?"

She shrugged and settled back, feeling a small bit of relief for the first time in weeks. Ever since Willy had cornered her at a bakery around the corner from her office, she'd been wary and tense. "Because this location was one of the first hotels Felix and Pierce built. Jenna loves being close as well. There's a sentimentality to this location that we don't feel for the others." She smiled warmly as the three hundred room hotel came into view. "It's special."

"I get that," he said, nodding his head. But when she turned to look at him, hoping that he truly did understand, he was watching her, not the building.

Ava suspected that his attention meant something. But she didn't have time to figure it out because the limousine came to a stop. Before she stepped out, she turned back to him. "Thank you," she whispered.

She lifted her chin, digging deep to find that remaining morsel of confidence she had before some jerk criminal started threatening her and her family. "I don't know what you have on Mr. Zanika that is going to protect me and my siblings, but thank you."

Before she made a fool of herself, Ava stepped out of the limousine and hurried into the hotel. She didn't look around as she hurried through the elegant area. She needed to be alone, to take a few moments to process that Grant was in Seattle. That he was here and she'd just agreed to act as his "girlfriend" for the next couple of weeks.

"Are you okay?"

Ava looked up, startled to find Jenna standing in her office doorway. Ava straightened, nervously smoothing her red, wool skirt down over her hips. "Of course. Why do you ask?"

Jenna stepped into the room and Ava wondered why her sister wore such dull clothes. They fit her perfectly, but the cream sheath dress with pearls and matching heels were just...blah! Jenna was beautiful. Her long, dark hair was sleek and shiny. She always pulled it back into a chignon at the back of her neck. Even her simple, pearl earrings were mild. With just a little effort, Jenna could be stunning! She had the long, dark lashes, cat eyes, and wide mouth that every model dreamed of. She wasn't overly thin, and she was in great shape, with visible muscles on her arms and calves, the only skin that showed today.

Jenna shrugged slightly. "I don't know. You're usually on the tense side, but it seems worse than usual lately. Then you went on that mysterious trip for a couple of days, only telling us that you had something to do." She stepped further into Ava's office. "Now, you're no longer tense. In fact," she tilted her head quizzically, "you actually seem happy."

Ava's eyes widened. "Happy?"

Jenna smiled and the expression only increased her beauty. "Yes. Happy." She laughed, hugging the files she'd been holding against her chest. A moment later, she turned serious. "You haven't been happy in a long time." She took another tentative step forward. "So I was just...I don't know." She looked down at the carpet, then back up at Ava. "Are you? Happy, that is?"

Ava blinked, not sure how to respond. Jenna was always perfect, always on top of everything in her life. Jenna never allowed chaos to rule her days, while Ava's life was filled with chaotic colors and a thousand projects that helped her...forget. Forget Grant?

No, impossible!

She just preferred being busy.

"I'm..." she struggled to find the right word, but after she'd considered and rejected several adjectives, she just went with the easiest for the moment. "I'm happy, Jenna." She looked at her sister's intelligent blue eyes, wishing that Ava could finally be as brilliant and beautiful as her big sister. "Are you?"

Jenna burst out with a short, almost bitter laugh. "Of course." She looked around, as if suddenly noting her surroundings before bringing her eyes back to Ava's. "Yes. We're all happy. We've 'made it', haven't we?"

Ava's thoughts traveled back to their first hotel, the little roadside dump they'd inherited from their mother. Comparing that place to their current surroundings, they should be happy.

"Yes. We're extremely happy," Ava confirmed.

A noise in the doorway interrupted their "happy" confirmations. "Jenna, do you have the budgets for the London conferences?" Pierce asked, stepping into Ava's office. Their older brother looked at Ava, then at Jenna, his dark eyebrows furrowing in concern. "What's going on? What's wrong?"

Jenna smiled and patted Pierce's shoulder. "We were just discussing how happy we were," she explained.

Pierce looked at each of them again, clearly unconvinced. "What's wrong?" he repeated.

Jenna laughed and turned, heading out of Ava's office. "I'll get you the budgets. I increased them by four percent because..." her voice trailed off as she rounded the corner. Ava watched as Pierce frowned at her. He obviously wanted to say something, but wasn't sure what to say. He sighed, rubbed his forehead, then turned on his heel and left Ava's office.

Poor Pierce, Ava thought, wishing that he could have some sort of break from the constant tension he must feel.

"Ava, we need the story boards for the newest marketing campaign," her marketing director asked, stepping into Ava's office and interrupting her concerns about her oldest brother.

Ava snapped back to the present. There was no point dwelling on the past and happiness was...well, it was a state of mind. She might not be happy, she thought, handing over the story boards she'd worked up last night after she'd gotten home. But she was...content. Yes, that was a good word. She was content.

If a spark of excitement continually interrupted her concentration over the rest of the afternoon, she ignored it. That spark had nothing to do with thoughts of Grant. He was a blast from the past, so to speak. He was only here to help her with a sticky, potentially disastrous, issue and he had some business in Seattle. That was it. Nothing more.

Grant stared thoughtfully out the window, wondering...? Would Ava like this house? Located in the North Capitol Hill area, the old house was well maintained with all of the modern conveniences, but had somehow managed to retain the quirky attitude from when it was built over a hundred years ago.

Ava would look perfect in this house. She was quirky and beautiful, vivacious, but also cautious. Would she like this house? Or would she prefer something more modern? Would she like the nooks and crannies of an older house? Or the sleek, clean lines of something contemporary.

He didn't know. And that bothered him. Would he ever find out?

"The neighborhood has excellent schools, if you're thinking about starting a family in the future."

The real estate agent's question instantly caused him to picture Ava pregnant, round and glowing with their child. He almost groaned at the image. She would be a beautiful mother, he thought.

And he definitely wanted to practice the art of making babies. But only with Ava.

After seeing her in Houston two days ago, he'd accepted that there had never been any other woman for him. Oh, he'd been with other women, but the interactions had been merely sexual. And none had come close to what he'd experienced eight years ago with Ava.

She was the one for him.

So now it was time to do what he did with everything else he'd wanted in his life. He needed to figure out a way to get her.

"Do you have any questions?" the agent asked. "Or would you like to see some other houses? Perhaps in a different neighborhood?"

Grant wondered where Ava lived now. For some reason, he couldn't picture her anywhere but in that tiny room at that run-down hotel where she'd grown up, running barefoot through the woods.

She wore shoes now. He loved the shoes she wore! The red heels from the other day were his favorite, but he wouldn't mind making love to Ava while she kept the black spike heels she'd had on earlier today. They were pretty darn nice. He wondered if she had any peep toe shoes. Or heeled sandals? Yeah, he'd like to see her in those too. Maybe wearing a bright, flowered sundress that hugged her pert, perfect breasts?

"Sir?"

Grant swung around, startling the agent. "I'll think about it," he told her, then walked out of the house. He couldn't commit to buying a new house until he better understood this current version of Ava. He just hoped there were some remnants of the old Ava buried underneath all of those cautious layers he sensed now.

He ignored the agent's startled, and disappointed, expression as he slipped back into the limousine. He needed a car, he thought. It was fine to have a driver for now. But he didn't like being driven around all the time. In Houston, he had several cars, but used a service for the nights when he needed more flexibility. He'd have to get his vehicles shipped up here to Seattle. No, maybe he would sell them and get something new and more practical. Seattle's weather was dramatically different from Houston's heat and humidity.

He'd never shied away from a challenge before. However, winning Ava was going to be the most difficult thing he'd ever done. Their past...he didn't understand why she hadn't come with him all those years ago. But now they were different people. Or were they?

He didn't know, but he was looking forward to finding out.

Chapter 5

Ava stared at the message on her phone. *Tonight at six. Cocktail dress.* That's all Grant had texted. Not the location of where they were going, nor the purpose of the evening. Would they be eating? Or should she get something to eat before he picked her up? How late would they be out? Were they going with others? Or meeting his business associates at the destination?

Her fingers hesitated over the buttons on her phone, but the questions simply wouldn't come. Or more specifically, her thoughts were whirling at top speed, going too fast for her to type out only one question. There were a zillion questions flitting through her head.

And yet, just the thought of seeing Grant tonight sent sparkles of sunshine through her system. It was another dreary, overcast day in Seattle with rain threatening on the horizon. What was new? But in her head, the clouds were gone and she was excited by the idea of spending some time with a man who...what? What did Grant do?

He was just a man, she reminded herself.

And yet, she glanced at the clock. It was already five o'clock? She leapt to her feet, grabbed her purse, and rushed out of her office.

"Ava?" her assistant, Dean, called out, concern and confusion in his voice.

"Gotta go!" Ava called back as she hustled past.

"But...you never leave before seven o'clock!" he called back.

Ava laughed as she jabbed at the elevator call button. "I know. Crazy, right?"

Dean's mouth literally fell open as she danced into the elevator.

"What's the occasion?" a deep, male voice asked.

Ava swung around, then laughed at Felix, who was lounged against the back wall of the elevator. "Felix!" she gasped, then threw herself at him. His arms enveloped her in a bear hug as he chuckled. "You're back!" she breathed, hugging him with all her strength. "I can't believe you're really here!"

Felix laughed, leaning back to look down at her. He was four inches over six feet, which meant that he literally towered over her. Pierce was nearly as tall, but Felix had an additional inch on their oldest brother, as well as Grant.

"What are you doing in Seattle? I thought you were still working on the Chicago site."

"I'm ahead of schedule and Pierce called me, asking about something odd. I decided to fly back and investigate in person." He looked her over carefully. "You look happy. Are you finally happy?"

"Finally?" she repeated, baffled. "Why do you say it like that?"

He tweaked her nose, something he'd done ever since she'd been a little kid and he was a gangly teen. "Because you always look sad, squirt."

She laughed, hugged him again, then straightened as the elevator doors opened to the parking garage. "I'm fine," she told him, not bothering to tell him she was happy. Why was everyone asking her that lately? She wasn't ever *unhappy*!

"You sure?" he asked, his expression turning serious. Those blue eyes, so familiar, and yet, so different, stared down at her. "You haven't been okay lately."

Had everyone suspected something was wrong? Damn, that stupid Willy Zanika!

Putting on an airy attitude, she stepped out of the elevator, pulling her car keys out as she waved to him. "Oh, just lots going on."

Felix put a hand to the doors of the elevators, stopping them from closing. "You'd tell me if something was wrong though, right?"

She smiled, her shoulders relaxing as she nodded. "Of course I'd tell you." She waved her keys in the air. "Gotta go."

Ava turned away, hurrying towards her car. It was a small, black, sporty model that she'd splurged on several years ago. It had been one of her first big purchases after they'd started to make a profit on the hotels. She sighed, slipping into the driver's seat. Those first few years had been difficult, but things were okay now. Everything was going to be fine.

Her excitement and anticipation for the upcoming evening was a bad thing, she told herself as she drove through the congested streets of downtown Seattle. And yet, no matter how much she tried to convince herself to moderate her eagerness, her heart still pounded and her stomach flipped at the thought of seeing Grant tonight.

As soon as she pulled into the driveway of her small, craftsman style house, she raced up the hardwood stairs to shower and change. She didn't have long to get ready and, since she wasn't sure what tonight's event was about, Ava wanted to find something neutral to wear. If he'd told her they were going sailing, she had an outfit for that. If he'd said they were having dinner with business acquaintances, she could do herself up ala Jenna and be conservative, but with a spark of something interesting. But the vague description of "cocktail dress" wasn't explicit enough.

However, as soon as she reached into her closet, she found her perfect "little black dress". The excellent black wool had a soft sheen to it, but the design of the dress cinched in at her waist and cupped her small breasts, making them appear larger and more lush. The neckline was high, the hem ended just above her knees, but the way the material clung to her made the dress sexier than it seemed while on a hangar.

Ava quickly did her makeup, leaving it minimal with mauve lipstick. She'd save her red lipstick for other events because it was her favorite.

The doorbell ringing made her heart leap and it took a moment for Ava to calm herself down. She fluffed her hair one more time, and grabbed the black dress, slipping it up over her hips and shoulders and hurried down the stairs with black stilettos in hand as she tried to pull up the zipper of her dress with the other.

"Just a minute!" she called out, twisting desperately. But it was no use. Her fingers were shaking too hard to grab the small zipper that was now stuck right between her shoulder blades.

Sighing, she leaned against the door, gazing up at the ceiling as she contemplated her options. She needed help. And again, Grant was the only person that came to mind. Okay, so he came to mind at the moment because he was standing on the other side of her front door. Still, she felt foolish that she couldn't even zip up her dress.

"Ava?" he called out.

Ava closed her eyes for a moment, then resigned herself to her fate. If she'd calmed down enough before pulling on this dress, she wouldn't be in this predicament. Sighing, she turned around and jerked the door open, glaring up at Grant as if this was all his fault.

Grant stared at her, trying to catch his breath. She looked...stunning! Ava had always been beautiful to him, even when they were just sitting by a creek in the dappled sunshine in worn, cutoff jeans. But tonight, the black dress and her long, dark hair streamed down over her shoulders like a dark cascade. She looked...amazing! Truly the most beautiful woman he'd ever known.

"I need help."

The three words jerked him back to the present and he looked around for the threat. "What's wrong?" he demanded, ready to charge in and slay whatever dragons threatened her.

Instead of a dragon, Ava turned her back to him, revealing pale, beautiful skin as well as the black band of her bra. She hadn't zipped up her dress! Was this an invitation?

She pulled all of that glorious, dark hair out of the way and glanced at him over her shoulder. "The zipper is stuck on something and I can't get it loose. Will you help me?"

Damn! She needed him to zip her up. She wasn't suggesting that he pull the zipper down.

Soon, he told himself. Very soon, she would be singing a different tune.

For the moment, he needed to get his body back under control. It was just a back, he told himself. A beautiful back, but still....

And yet, he struggled to remember that she needed him to pull the zipper up and not down.

"The zipper is jammed." He stepped forward, taking the zipper pull while trying not to touch her. But it was no use. The material was caught in the zipper's teeth and it took some effort to get it unstuck. The backs of his fingers brushed against her skin. If that was all that happened in that moment, he could have handled it. But Ava shivered and, because his fingers were right there, and he was looking down over her shoulder, he saw the heat steal into her cheeks, showing him that the brush of his fingers affected her just as much as it had affected him.

The zipper came unstuck after another tug and he pulled the zip all the way up her back, then settled his hands onto her shoulders. "Better?" he asked.

She wasn't wearing her shoes, so she seemed shorter than usual. Or perhaps it was just her personality that made her seem so large most of the time. Ava was a spitfire that attacked life head on.

Which only made her current situation, and his presence back in her life, all the more dire. She needed his help. Grant had vowed he wouldn't make love to Ava until he'd resolved the issue of Zanika plaguing her.

Remembering that vow, he let his hands drop to his sides and stepped back. "All fixed," he told her as she turned around. Damn, she was a tiny thing!

"Thank you," Ava replied. She smiled slightly up at him, but her eyes only lifted to his chin. Then she bent down and he almost groaned out loud as he watched her slip on her shoes. Ava's dress was tight enough that she had to do that side-bending thing. The movement made her legs look extra-long. Plus, he loved the way her toes slipped into the shoe first, then her heel. She straightened, then slipped on the other shoe.

When she straightened again, Grant mocked himself. Of course the woman put her toes into the shoe first! What an idiot! Was there another way to do that? Perhaps heel first? He was being ridiculous.

"You look nice," he replied.

Ava looked down again, grabbing her purse. It was a cute little thing that he doubted could hold more than the absolute basics. Sure enough, she walked over to the black, leather tote bag she normally carried and pulled out her small wallet, then looked at the small, gold "jewelry box" looking purse. The wallet fit, but when she tried to add her lipstick, there was no more room.

"I'll carry that for you," he offered, plucking the lipstick from her grasp. He slid it into the pocket of his suit jacket, swallowing a chuckle at her horrified expression. So the little spitfire didn't like being out of control? Interesting.

"Are you ready?"

Ava looked around, grabbed her house keys, and nodded. "Ready," she replied with a nod. "You haven't told me where we're going tonight."

She tried very hard to keep her eyes off Grant's dark suit. It wasn't a tuxedo, but the material, like her dress, was a touch more formal than a business suit. Mentally, she was cursing herself for choosing something that matched perfectly, even by accident. As they walked down the three steps from her front porch to the short sidewalk leading to her driveway, she realized that his black tie and crisp, white dress shirt next to her black dress and the double strand of pearls she'd chosen for the evening, looked like they'd coordinated their outfits. Like they'd dressed together before heading out for the night.

Shaking that thought away, she forced her lips into a semblance of a smile as she thanked him for opening the door to the limousine. Why a limousine? Did the man not enjoy driving? Ava loved to drive. She loved the freedom it gave her.

"Why did you hire a limousine? The traffic can be rough at times, but it's not nearly as bad as Los Angeles or Washington, D.C."

He shrugged, adjusting his jacket as he settled into the seat beside her. "I like the freedom it gives me. I don't have to worry about parking and it's just easier when I'm not as familiar with the city streets." He turned and looked at her, his lips curled up at the sides slightly. "Do you think

I don't know how to drive?"

She fought to keep from laughing. "I know you are an excellent driver, Grant."

He chuckled as old memories surfaced. "Ah! The old pickup truck."

She laughed at the memory as well. "I don't know how you managed to get that rusted heap of rotting parts to work again. How long had it been in that old barn?"

He laughed. "I would guess at least twenty years. But it was such an old vehicle, the only parts that needed to be replaced were the rubber timing belts."

"And the seats!" she countered, shaking her head. "That roll of duct tape really wasn't adequate protection."

He lifted a dark eyebrow. "I thought that taping up the ripped vinyl seats was pretty genius. It worked, didn't it? All of those wire coils were covered."

"Barely!" she chimed in, smiling. "I really don't know why you spent so much time trying to fix that thing."

"Don't you?" he asked, gazing down at her meaningfully.

Ava lifted her eyes, staring into his as those memories flashed back to her. "Because...?"

"I worked on that rusty heap because, every time I came around, a cute young woman with adorable braids and the hottest pair of cut-off jean shorts perched on the bumper. It was a great way to get you to talk to me."

Her jaw dropped. "Are you seriously telling me that the work you did fixing that old truck was a cover just to talk to me?"

He shrugged those magnificent shoulders. "Yes."

That was a startling answer and Ava wasn't sure how to respond. She looked up at him, then quickly away, unable to deal with the intensity of his gaze.

Clearing her throat, she tried to change the subject. "What happened to that truck?"

"I sold it. I actually got several thousand dollars for it since I was able to rebuild the engine."

For some reason, that hurt. Why would she be hurt that he'd sold a truck that...well, it had meant something to her only because he'd worked on it. Grant had been the one to find the old truck and figured out how to fix it, make it purr.

Ignoring the pain lashing at her chest, she forced her lips to smile as she offered, "That truck was a bit like the way you work, wasn't it?"

"What do you mean?"

She smiled. "You find businesses that need help. Just like the truck."

He shrugged. "The old Ford truck was a collector's item after it was running again. I sold that truck and bought a convenience store in downtown Chicago. That shop was about to go out of business because the owner was too old and the employees were stealing. I fired everyone, worked on training a new staff, refreshed the inventory, then sold the store for ten times the amount I bought it for six months later to a family that still owns it. The store is thriving now."

She smiled, impressed with his business strategy. "That's what you do, right? You take businesses that are failing, fix them up, make them profitable, and then sell it to someone who wants to run the business long term?"

"Yes. That's my strategy. It's worked so far. And I enjoy the challenge of figuring out why a business is failing and finding ways to make it profitable again."

She nodded. "What company are you looking at now?"

He chuckled. "Right now, I'm in the middle of fixing Testone Industries."

Her eyes widened. "I heard that someone had bought that company. I was just about to sell my stock when I heard that it was going to be bought up, but I didn't realize that you were behind the "white knight" effort."

"I try to keep my company's involvement more circumspect lately."

"Why is that?" she asked. "I would have thought that your efforts would be widely publicized. Why would you keep your interest a secret?"

He considered her question for a moment and Ava wondered what he wasn't going to say. "I've discovered that, if I even *look* at a company, and don't step in to fix things, then the stigma to the company is too great for the current owners to survive."

Ava understood what he was saying and it gave her a stab of pride. "You've become too well known within the business industry, eh?" she teased. "People think that your interest in a company is going to be the saving grace, and if you reject buying it, then there's no hope for the business?"

He huffed a little, and muttered, "Something like that."

She laughed and he glowered at her, but that only made her amusement grow. "Oh, give over, Grant! You're a victim of your own success. You're renowned within the industry for being the man who comes in and saves a company. Looking at a business is synonymous with something being wrong, either with the management or the products it sells. Just revel in your success."

He mumbled something unintelligible, but the limousine came to a stop outside of a restaurant. "What's this?" she asked.

"It's a grand opening for a friend," he explained as he stepped out, then turned to help her out onto the sidewalk. "I told her that I would show up and lend my name to the opening." He sighed with frustration. "She seems to think that my being here will bring more..."

He trailed off as a contingent of reporters hustled over, jockeying to get a photograph of him. Grant put an arm around Ava, pulling her against his side protectively while he smothered several expletives.

"What's going on?" Ava hissed up to him, her soft curves pressing against him and forcing him to grit his teeth to keep his body's reaction under control.

"I'm sorry, Ava. I didn't realize that Debra would call in this level of publicity."

Ava forced a smile, remembering her advice to her brother during press mobs. Just smile and endure until you are safely away, she used to tell him. "If you look dumb-struck, they'll think you're dumb."

Pasting an image of confidence on her face, she waved to the paparazzi, walking alongside Grant as he maneuvered both of them through the mass of photographers that were screaming his name, and hers as soon as they realized who she was.

When they were finally inside the crowded restaurant, mingling with other guests, she let out a breath and shook herself, both physically and mentally. "Well, that was unexpected."

"I'm sorry, Ava," he said, looking down at her carefully. "Are you okay? Are you hurt in any way?"

"No!" she assured him. "I'm fine. I've advised Pierce and Felix on this type of issue, as well as several celebrities that stayed in our hotels over the years. I know how to handle myself in front of the press, although I've never had to deal with it myself." She laughed it off, but deep inside, she cringed with the horror of being caught unaware like that.

Carefully, Ava lifted a hand to touch the pearls at her throat, grateful that she'd taken such pains with her appearance tonight. Of course, she'd done it to impress Grant, not because of the press.

"Grant!" a beautiful blond woman called out.

Ava and Grant turned as a woman dressed in a shimmering gold cocktail dress pushed her way through the crowd towards them, her arms wide. The woman in question didn't hesitate to embrace Grant, which meant that Ava was literally shoved out of the way. "Oh, it's so good of you to come tonight! I'm so excited that you are taking a chance with my new business endeavor and lending me your name for the opening!"

The woman shifted her body, looping both arms through Grant's. She chose his right arm, the same arm that had, moments before, been wrapped around Ava's waist. Ava gritted her teeth as her temper simmered.

Stepping back, Ava watched the two interact. They'd been lovers, she realized with a stabbing pain in her chest. Heartless bastard, she thought in disgust, and walked away. Carefully, she made her way through the crowd to the bar and smiled at the bartender. He immediately stepped away from the other group and walked over to her, offering her a charming grin.

"What can I get you?" the man asked.

Ava smiled at him, needing the confidence boost after being so callously abandoned.

"I'll have a glass of white wine, please. Just whatever is open." She wasn't going to actually drink it. Not this time! She was painfully aware of the last time she drank wine around Grant. However, she needed something in her hands, as well as a bit of liquid courage to get through the night. She wasn't going to stay, but nor was she going to run away with her tail between her legs simply because Grant had abandoned her.

"You got it, love," the bartender, a handsome guy in his early twenties, called out, grabbing a glass while winking at her.

Ava wasn't impressed. All of the Halliday Hotel bartenders were trained to be professional at all times. They were not allowed to flirt with the customers. This bartender would have been fired immediately.

But she went along with it for the moment if it meant that she'd get her glass of wine faster.

The man placed the glass on the bar counter with a flourish as Ava pulled out her wallet, prepared to pay for the drink.

"On the house, love," he said, giving her another wink. "If you need anything else, just call for me. My name is Danny and I'm at your service."

Another mark against him, she thought. Giving away free drinks was an absolute no-no. Vaguely, Ava wondered if she should mention the poor employee training to the blond goddess. Was she still clinging to Grant?

"Why did you leave me?" the man in question asked, having come up behind her.

Ava turned away, unwilling to give him any slack after what he'd just done.

"You had your hands full with your lover."

"Debra is not my lover," he growled, signaling to the bartender.

Ava smirked as Danny pretended to ignore Grant, and took a sip of her wine. "Former lover, then. Whatever."

Grant turned and glared down at her. "Debra and I haven't been together for years."

She rolled her eyes. "I don't think that *Debra*," she snarled the name, "thinks that your relationship is over. If so, she wouldn't have pushed me out of the way like that." She turned and walked away.

Grant grabbed her arm, pulling her back to his side. "She's nothing to me now, Ava. I promise."

Ava was only mildly appeased. Especially when Debra laughed loudly at something someone said, then pointed towards Grant as if she were heading towards him again.

"Your lover is on the way again. Brace yourself. She doesn't look like she took your previous brush off to heart."

Grant glanced over, realized that Ava was right, that Debra was indeed heading straight for him again. He took Ava's glass of wine, set it on the bar, and took her now-empty hand. "We're getting out of here," he snapped, literally pulling her through the crowd. Because of his size and, most likely, the expression on his face, the guests quickly moved out of the way. He pushed through the front door of the restaurant, startling the waiting paparazzi that weren't expecting anyone to leave so suddenly. He was able to pull her into a restaurant directly across the street before they were able to catch up with them.

"I don't have a reservation," Grant snarled to the maitre'd. "Any chance that you have an open table?"

The man stiffened slightly, eyed Grant more closely, looked out the window at the crowd of reporters who were waving their cameras, trying to get pictures of Grant and Ava through the windows, then back at Grant. "Absolutely, sir," he said, grabbing two menus from the podium. "Right this way."

"Good evening, Ms. Halliday," the waitress bowed slightly to Ava, then turned to Grant, "and Mr. Hanover. What can I get you to drink tonight?"

"Ms. Halliday will have a glass of white wine and I'll have a glass of scotch."

"Very good sir," she bowed again. "Would you like to hear the chef's specials?"

"No!" they said at the same time.

The waitress, startled, smiled professionally, and backed away saying, "I'll get your drinks and will be right back to take your order."

Alone again, Ava glared at him. "How long were you with her?"

"Who?" Grant demanded.

"The gold woman!" she hissed, unable to tamp down her jealousy any longer.

"Debra?"

Ava rolled her eyes, leaning back in the chair and crossing her arms over her chest. "Was there another woman draped in tacky, gold lame that accosted you tonight?"

He sighed, rubbing a hand over the back of his neck. "No, I suppose you're right." He hesitated briefly. "Why do you want to know about Debra? She and I were together a long time ago."

"As I said, I don't think Debra believes the two of you are over."

Grant sighed and started to speak, but the waitress arrived with their drinks. She obviously felt the tension because she set their drinks down and hurried away without offering to take their orders.

Visibly frustrated, Grant leaned forward, "Look, I know that Debra was rude to you tonight, but there's no reason to be jealous of her. I told you, Debra and I were over a long time ago."

Ava leaned her elbows on the table, ignoring the etiquette that Jenna had drilled into her. "Like I said," she retorted, her tone dripping with sarcasm, "I don't think *she* believes that. And I'm not going to be brushed aside like last night's crumbs. Not by you or anyone."

He was silent for a long moment, then slowly, Grant nodded. "Understood. I won't ever allow anyone else to brush you aside while we're together."

With that, he picked up his menu and perused, ignoring Ava's gaping jaw.

"I didn't mean...you aren't...!" she glanced around, hoping that they weren't disturbing the other diners. She'd had enough of being a spectacle tonight. Thankfully, the other diners weren't paying attention to them. "Grant, we *are not* a couple."

He laid the menu down. "Of course we *are* a couple. For as long as it takes to get Zanika to leave you, your family, and your business alone, you and I are together."

She opened her mouth to argue, but the dratted waitress arrived. Did the woman have to be so efficient?

"So, what can I get for you tonight?" she asked with a politely blank expression, even though it was obvious that the two diners were in mental combat.

Grant snapped his menu closed. "I'll have the steak with garlic risotto. Ms. Halliday will have the scallops and shrimp."

Ava glared at him, trying to work up the steam to contradict him. But she absolutely loved seafood and he knew it. She should probably be happy that he remembered, as well as the fact that he'd bothered to check the menu for something that she would enjoy. But at the moment, she was still too...too...what? What *was* she feeling at the moment? It certainly wasn't jealousy! She couldn't feel jealousy! She was cool and collected! She was the cold fish that too many of her previous boyfriends had accused her of being!

She closed her menu as well, forcing her lips to curl into a smile as she handed the menu back to the waitress who immediately rushed away.

"What just went through your mind?" Grant asked, his voice gentle. Almost as if he cared.

Ava's lashes lowered and she shook her head. "Nothing. I'm fine."

He sighed and she glanced up at him. "I'm fine," she reiterated more firmly.

He shook his head. "You're not fine, Ava. You're angry with me." His gaze narrowed on her and he was silent for another moment, and then took a sip of his scotch. "Will you tell me what you've been up to since we last saw each other?" he asked. He waved his glass slightly. "Besides the obvious."

"What's the obvious?" she asked, imitating him by taking another sip of her wine before setting it carefully back down on the table then picking up her glass of ice water and taking a longer sip.

"Working with your siblings to build up an impressive hotel empire," he replied. "I've followed the Halliday success. It's extraordinary."

She nodded, setting the water glass down with precision. "Pierce has done an outstanding job of guiding the financial success of the hotels. He seems to have a knack for finding the best places to build the next hotel, or knowing which hotel chain is in trouble and whittling down the owner's price to something that is reasonable." Ava fiddled with her napkin, carefully spreading it out over her lap. "Jenna is a whiz at managing the details. She's great at hiring excellent employees too. And Felix, even before he got out of the Navy, he just seemed to know how to build things."

"How in the world did he help the growth of the hotel while he was in the Navy? Wasn't he a SEAL?"

She laughed, relaxing now that the conversation wasn't about her anymore. "Yes. Felix was impressive as a Navy SEAL. He loved the adventure and the challenge of keeping up with his team. He even got his degree in mathematics while on the SEAL team, although I have absolutely no idea how he managed it, since sometimes he was gone for several weeks at a time on a mission."

"I can't imagine that either. I'll have to ask him some day."

She grinned. "If you can tease the story out of him, would you please tell me?"

"Absolutely."

Their dinner arrived and Ava suddenly realized how hungry she was.

"Oh, this looks delicious."

The waitress smiled as she set their plates down, then walked away, leaving them to their conversation.

"You were telling me how Felix helped build the business while in the Navy."

She swallowed a bite of perfectly cooked scallop, then nodded, wiped her mouth and explained. "Felix somehow coerced his teammates into spending their holidays at the old, roadside hotel site. Then he'd show them his drawings, the things he wanted to build. Navy SEALs aren't very good at relaxing, I've learned. So they'd spend one, maybe two days relaxing by the lake, then Felix would gather them all up and they'd build extra cabins or add on a wild looking deck to each of the existing cabins. Because Navy SEALs are a little nuts to begin with, the decks and the newest cabins were always better than the last ones they'd built." She grinned at the memory. "Those cabins really were what put us on the map. We were able to charge outrageous prices for a round tree cabin or an upside down triangle cabin." She shook her head. "To this day, I still don't know how some of those cabins remain standing, but every one of them is booked solidly for the next eighteen months." She stabbed a braised shrimp. "Jenna used to allow reservations further into the future for those sixty cabins, but people started to complain that they couldn't get a booking. So she limited the reservations to eighteen months in the future. I have no idea why that stopped the complaints, but it did."

"And you do all of the decorating for these cabins?"

She grinned, trying to hide the burst of pride at her accomplishments. "Yeah. I do all of the décor for every hotel we bring under the Halliday label."

"But you don't think that your efforts have anything to do with the success?"

She snorted. "Marketing is simple. I take pictures of the cabins or the hotels, the pools, the sunsets...whatever. People really like my designs of the bars, for whatever reason. I take pictures, post them online, and get the word out. People find the hotels' websites and call for reservations." She stabbed another scallop. "It's more about the location of the hotel and the excellent staff than the décor."

"I doubt it, but that's revealing in itself." Before she could ask what that meant , he changed the subject. "What part do you like the best? The decorating or the marketing?"

She waved his comment aside. "It doesn't matter. They gave me the easy stuff to do." She sighed, no longer hungry. Putting her fork down, she looked up at him. "What do you look for when evaluating a company? Is there a formula you use? Or do you mostly go by instinct?"

He didn't answer for a moment. He looked at her for so long, Ava wondered if he was going to answer her at all. Thankfully, he nodded. "Yes. Both. I have a formula, an evaluation process, so to speak. But when I'm speaking with business owners or the leaders of the various companies, I also evaluate them as well as the staff. That part is mostly by instinct, I suppose."

She smiled at him, admiring him even more. "That's fascinating."

"You don't think that you go with instincts in the work you do?"

She snorted. "Of course not."

"You don't have a formula for decorating the hotels? I've seen them and each one is very different, but there's a certain flair that is recognizable."

She shrugged and stabbed another scallop. "I spend a week in each city where I'm going to decorate. I get a feel for the city and then choose three colors. When I start decorating the hotel, I work with those three colors to develop a theme. Sometimes the colors change as I work on the design and other times, I'm pretty much on target and the color scheme seems to fit the culture of the city."

He nodded, cutting into the steak. "That's instinct. But there's more to designing than just color. Your hotels are well balanced and coordinated."

She shrugged, then waved her hand dismissively in the air. "That's because of Felix. He knows how to put a column in exactly the right place, a fountain in the front or the back, maybe even off to the side."

"But you're the one that designs around those columns and courtyards. You're the one that makes each space special." He tilted his head slightly. "Why do you keep diminishing your contribution?"

"Because decorating is easy," she said with exasperation and set her fork down impatiently. "Anyone could do it."

"I can't," he argued. "I can't combine colors and designs. I hire someone to decorate my house and my offices spaces. I also hire people to come in and formulate efficient work spaces sometimes, when needed."

She waved her fork in the air. "I'll accept that work spaces need to be efficient. But seriously, the success of Halliday Hotels is mostly due to my siblings."

He stared at her for a long moment, then asked, "Do you still go out into the woods with your camera and take pictures?"

This was dangerous territory. Her photography was highly personal. No one knew about her private hobby, although she'd planned to put some of her pieces into the art exhibit. Not under her own name though. Not a chance!

"I still dabble, but not as often as I used to."

"Why is that? From what I remember, you were very good."

She shrugged. "I enjoy the process, but there are plenty of better photographers out there."

She sipped her wine, feeling uncomfortable under the intensity of his gaze. "What do you do for a hobby?"

He finished off his steak and lifted his glass of water, draining it before he answered her. "I don't have time for hobbies. Work takes up a great deal of my time."

"That's a pity. I think everyone should have a hobby." She was about to say something more when their surprisingly pleasant conversation was interrupted.

"Ava Halliday!" a sneering voice called out.

Ava froze. After a moment, she turned, forcing her lips into a tight smile. "Bessie. What a...surprise!"

Bessie Tourmaine was Ava's high school nemesis. She'd been the high school cheerleader, the girl who'd gotten all the guys. She hadn't been especially smart in class, and had always seemed to compete with Ava for some reason. Bessie had been from the "right" side of the tracks. Literally. Bessie's family had one of the largest homes in the small town outside of Seattle where they'd grown up.

"And Grant Hanover!" Her syrupy smile turned predatory. "Well, isn't this an amazing surprise!" she breathed, leaning against Ava's chair as if Ava was no longer sitting in it.

Grant stood up, politely taking the woman's hand. "I don't think we've met."

Bessie laughed, putting a hand to her chest. "Oh, you were the man about town that everyone noticed. Even better," she purred, letting her eyes move over Grant's broad shoulders as her smile widened. "you were the guy that every girl wanted, but no one ever quite managed to catch your eye. Isn't that right, Ava?" she asked pointedly.

Ava didn't bother to answer, knowing that Bessie didn't care about her response.

Bessie leaned more heavily against Ava's chair. Ava wondered what would happen if she stood up. Would Bessie hit the floor? Oh, wouldn't that be a lovely sight!

Grant clearly noticed because he said mildly, "Bessie, would you mind giving Ava some breathing room? I don't think that she's comfortable with you looming over her like that."

Bessie jumped theatrically and glanced down at Ava as if she'd entirely forgotten that she was there. "Oh! I'm so sorry!" she yelped in feigned surprise. "Silly me!" she cooed, moving her hand to Grant's chair. Ava wanted to poke the woman's eye out. But the woman turned her attention right back to Grant. "So, what brings you to Seattle, Grant? Are you looking to buy another company and make another hugely delicious profit?"

Grant's features were shuttered, but Ava could see the revulsion in his eyes. "I always keep my options open."

The woman laughed and Ava cringed. Unfortunately, Bessie didn't have soft, tingling laughter; she had a grating, harsh sound, like a faulty engine.

Grant didn't bother to hide his disdain. He looked directly at Bessie and said, "If you'll excuse us, Ava and I are having a private dinner."

Bessie laughed again. "Oh, Ava won't mind if we chat a bit longer."

"I would," he snapped, his tone hard and uncompromising.

Startled by Grant's blunt dismissal, Bessie blinked. She waited for a long moment, her smile frozen awkwardly on her overly made up face. Then she frowned down at Ava. "Got it!" She sighed dramatically and shifted slightly, giving Grant a better angle to ogle her figure in a tight dress. "Well, I'll just toddle off then, but maybe we could have dinner soon. Just the two of us. And we can get to know one another without...distractions, shall we?"

Bessie moved off before Grant could discourage her further, walking towards an older, balding man with a protruding stomach who was obviously waiting for her.

Grant finally sat down, shaking his head. "Friend of yours?"

"Enemy, more like it."

Grant seemed to shudder. "She doesn't seem to be a fan."

"Nope. For some reason, Bessie competed against me for everything during our high school years, even though she seemed to have it all."

"Have you finished eating?" he asked. "We still need to go over the plan for Zanika."

"Right," she sighed and nodded. "Yes. I'm done." She lifted her hand to get the waitress' attention. "I'll pay the–"

"Not a chance," he argued, tossing several bills on the table before coming around to her side of the table. "Let's go."

Chapter 6

"You should have seen her!" Bessie hissed, settling in Willy's lap.

"Seen who?" Willy demanded, irritated by the woman's voice, but enjoying the curve of her ass as she wiggled. His hand moved from the cut-crystal glass to her breast, kneading the soft flesh. Bessie was his favorite flavor of woman, he thought, pushing away the image of another woman, a classier, more refined woman with long, brown hair and a hot body. Ava Halliday wasn't ready for him. Yet. He'd eventually get the bitch into his bed, if only to satisfy his curiosity about what it would be like. Bessie though...he eyed the low cut of her red dress... Bessie was the kind who enjoyed sex, who would do anything he told her to do, even if it was the nastiest, most crude idea he could come up with. In fact, the cruder, the better for her.

"That Halliday brat!" Bessie shrilled. "Aren't you listening to me?" she demanded, smacking his hand off of her breast.

Halliday? "Which Halliday brat?" he snapped.

"Ava! The youngest." Bessie's eyes narrowed on Willy's tight features. "Stop messing with my boobs and pay attention. If I wanted to be ignored, I'd go back to my husband, the bald bastard."

Willy chuckled, pushing her hand out of his way as he continued his exploration of her breast. "You won't get any satisfaction from that old fart, and we both know it, so stop threatening me with him."

Bessie humphed a bit, then snuggled against him. "Whatever." She tossed her head slightly, then offered him what she thought of as her sexy pout. "But you should have seen her tonight. God, I hate her! She was always such a priss back when we were at school. But now, she's even worse. Sitting across from that gorgeous man, as if she was too good even for him!"

That got Willy's attention! Ava Halliday was dining with some other man? What the hell? Willy had plans for her and yeah, he agreed that Ava was a bit of a priss. Willy considered that to be part of her allure. She was sophisticated and...well, there was a purity to her that appealed to his darker side. He had plans to marry Ava. She was like a shiny princess that he couldn't wait to tarnish. Or maybe not.

He looked down at Bessie's voluptuous body, soft in all the right places, with the delectable curves and dimples that he liked. Maybe he'd preserve Ava's purity and keep Bessie on the side for fun. Well, Bessie and some of the other women that he liked to visit whenever he was in the mood for something on the more...exotic... end of the sexual spectrum.

"Who the hell was Ava dining with tonight?" he demanded. Willy would visit the bastard tomorrow and have a little chat with him. He would explain that Ava Halliday was *his*, until he decided to either wed the bitch or just...well, he wasn't sure what he'd do with her. Maybe he would rough her up a bit. Yes, that definitely appealed to his darker side. Roughing up the prissy princess. He almost chuckled at the thought.

Bessie sneered and he considered slapping that expression off her face. "You weren't listening to me, were you?"

Willy pinched Bessie's nipple. Hard. He enjoyed her gasp of pain as the woman crumpled, her fingers clenching his wrist in a vain effort to make him let go.

"Grant!" she gasped, whimpering when she accepted that she wasn't going to get his hand away. "Grant Hanover!"

Willy released Bessie, but he also abruptly stood up, dumping Bessie onto her bottom at his feet. She cried out at the additional insult as well as the pain from her landing, but Willy stepped over her, oblivious to her fury.

Grant Hanover was back? When the hell had he returned to Seattle? And why? Sweat broke out on his forehead as he thought about the repercussions of Hanover being here.

Eight years! Hanover had stayed out of Willy's business for eight long years! They'd made a deal. Willy wouldn't interfere with Hanover's business efforts and Hanover would hide the damning evidence from the police.

He paced the expanse of his living room, kicking Bessie when she didn't move her legs out of his path fast enough. If Hanover were here, then did that mean...? Hell, he had no idea what that meant! But it couldn't be good.

There was only one thing to do. He'd visit Hanover and find out what was going on. If the bastard was going to release the evidence, then

Willy would just have to...find it and destroy it. Yes, that was a good plan. He'd find the damn file and get rid of it!

Why hadn't he put more energy into destroying that evidence long before now? Hanover had held that crap over his head for eight long years. Of course, the bastard had left town, which had eased Willy's concerns. But still, as a businessman, Willy should never have allowed someone to have power over him. That was just common sense.

"What the hell, Willie?" Bessie whined as he walked up the stairs to his bedroom.

"Go home!" he snapped, and even that order irritated him. Bessie was the kind of woman that should be able to get his mind off of his troubles. But what Hanover had on Willy was just too great to be ignored. He needed to come up with a plan.

Unfortunately, Willy couldn't trust his men to handle this situation. If they ever got hold of that evidence, then they'd use it to destroy him. Willy wasn't in the business of giving his subordinates power over him.

Perhaps his first visit should be to the lovely, ever so vulnerable Ms. Halliday. Damn, he loved seeing that look of terror in her eyes. Ava tried to hide her fear, but it was always there. And it turned him on!

Chapter 7

Ava walked down the hallway towards the main ballroom or conference room, depending on who was renting the space that day. It was really just a large, open room with elegant chandeliers and huge windows along one wall and doors that opened up onto a stone terrace that overlooked the garden restaurant on the lower level.

Ava adored this room. She'd designed it with a Victorian ballroom in mind. It had the lovely coffered ceilings and huge chandeliers, but the walls weren't as elaborate. She'd wanted the "wow" effect to come from the ceiling and windows. It was a dramatic effect that would be perfect for the exhibit. Unfortunately, she couldn't start setting up the art pieces yet since the space was completely rented for other events. She would be working late the night before the exhibit officially opens because there was a business conference during the day.

Sighing with happiness, she scribbled down a few more ideas, various ways to display the artists' paintings for more impact. This art exhibit was going to be beautiful!

She was so focused on her ideas that she didn't notice someone else enter the space. So it was a shock to hear the sneering, nasally voice behind her.

"Ah, my latest pet!" Willy Zanika sneered, not stopping until he was at her side, invading her personal space.

Ava cringed and backed away, almost gagging at the stench of garlic and onions on his breath. "What are you doing here?" she hissed.

"Why wouldn't I be here?" he snarled, dragging her closer to him again. "We have a business arrangement." His finger slid down over the skin left bare by her sleeveless dress. "Don't you remember?" He leaned forward and Ava almost choked, the smell of his breath was truly appalling. "Or should I remind you of our...agreement?"

Ava ripped her arm out of his grasp and put more space between them. "Don't touch me!" she snapped. "And no! There was never an agreement. Just an ultimatum. A threat!"

He chuckled softly, his pinched expression making his next words even more terrifying. "Yes, but a threat that I'm more than willing to follow through on. You haven't spoken to any of my...colleagues, have you? They will be more than happy to explain to you what happens when someone defies me."

Ava stared, her horror at his unspoken threat making her blood run cold.

Willy chuckled at her fear. "Oh, yes," he murmured soothingly, inching closer again. "We're going to have a lot of fun, you and me. I like it when my lovers are afraid of me." He sucked his tongue through his teeth, making a snapping sound. "It turns me on when they are terrified." He chuckled and rubbed a hand over his groin. "And if they *aren't* scared, then I..." he paused for a moment, his lips curling into a malicious smile, "then I like to whip them until they know what terror is." He let his eyes move over her body. "Would you like to be whipped, Ava?"

He stroked his finger down her arm again. "It isn't pretty." That finger moved to her hair, sliding the strands back so that he could see her crystal blue eyes more clearly. Could he see the hate? Could he see the revulsion? He chuckled, so that would be a yes to both questions. "You're a beautiful woman, Ava. I'd hate to see that pretty face...."

"Get your hands off her!" a commanding voice came from the doorway.

Both Ava and Willy turned, their eyes widening as they saw Grant striding down the long, wide room. His rage was so intense, it was like he was followed by a thundercloud. He glared at Willy as if he were vermin. Which he was!

"What the hell are you doing here! I thought your business was in Houston!"

Grant couldn't remember ever being so furious. He pulled Ava into his arms, pressing her against his far side, so he was between them. His anger cranked up several notches when he realized that Willy had touched Ava. By the terror in her eyes, Grant suspected the weasel had threatened her again.

"My business..." he hissed, pausing for emphasis, "is anywhere I want it to be. Right now, my business is here in Seattle. More specifically, my business is with Halliday Hotels and more specifically, Ava Halliday." He released Ava, pushing her gently behind him so that Willy couldn't even see her. He loomed threateningly over the smelly man. "I know that you are going to be a good boy and leave Ava and her family alone. Aren't you?"

Zanika bared his teeth like the rabid animal that he was. For a long moment, the two of them stared each other down, but Willy knew who was in charge here. He backed down with a little "snick" as he once again sucked the saliva between his teeth and gums.

"So...when did this little romance start?"

"Eight years ago," Grant snarled. "Get out of this building. And don't ever come back." Grant stepped even closer. "In fact, don't even walk the street around this hotel or any hotel within the Halliday umbrella. Do I make myself clear?"

Zanika made another noise, but Grant didn't blink. This was it. This was the showdown that they'd been expecting ever since the incident happened.

"I don't think you have it anymore," Zanika whispered. "I think you've lost it!" He kept his voice low, but it was still menacing.

Grant's lips curled into a slight smirk. "I'll email you a copy." Zanika's eyes widened and, finally, there was a hint of nervousness in those dark depths. "Would be a shame if the police were monitoring your email accounts, wouldn't it?"

Neither man spoke for another long moment. Finally, Zanika backed down, muttered a curse, and stalked away.

Grant sighed, released the tension in his shoulders, then turned to look for Ava. She'd been shaking like a leaf, damn it! Zanika had scared her! What the hell had Willy said to her before he'd arrived?

Unfortunately, Ava had vanished. Where the hell had she gone?

He made his way out of the hotel and into the executive offices. "I'd like to speak with Ava Halliday. I don't have an appointment," he explained to the receptionist sitting at the front.

The woman, a younger woman in her early twenties, very politely said, "I'm sorry but Ms. Halliday has left the office for the day."

Grant's gaze sharpened on her in alarm. "When? When did she leave?"

The receptionist's eyes widened at the urgency in his tone. She shrugged, then explained, "Just a moment ago. I know that she was inspecting the ballroom, but she came back looking...well, not well. She went to her office, grabbed her purse, and left."

Grant rubbed the bridge of his nose, then nodded. "Thank you." With that, he left the executive offices. He'd driven here this time, since two of his vehicles had been delivered from Houston late yesterday, so he ducked into the Lexus sedan and pulled into traffic. Ava had been trembling and then she'd run away from work. He had to go to her. He had to find out what Zanika said to her and reassure her.

Rushing to her house, he parked right behind her cute little black sports car. Scanning the house, he looked for signs that she was inside.

There was no movement outside, even though she had a lovely little set of chairs and small table for relaxing on the front porch. In the back of his mind, he wondered why she'd bought such a small house. He knew that she was very wealthy. Hell, she was part owner in an international hotel empire! She could afford just about any type of residence she wanted!

The last time he'd been here, to pick Ava up for their dinner at Debra's opening, Grant had only had eyes for Ava. Even walking up the short sidewalk now, he acknowledged that he hadn't noticed anything at the time because anticipation had blinded him completely.

Now, he noticed, but only because he was looking for Ava, as well as signs of her personality and wondering how he could help her get through the revulsion of having been touched by Zanika.

She scrubbed harder. Turning the water hotter, Ava frantically tried to wash away the filth left by Willy Zanika's touch. But she could still feel his fingers; still see his sneer when she closed her eyes.

The shaking was so bad now, she could barely remain standing. But Ava couldn't stop scrubbing. Her skin felt like it was crawling with bugs, or maybe germs and vile thoughts that the man had forced on her.

"Get off!" she shrieked, tossing the sponge away and using her fingernails to get rid of the sensations as panicked tears poured down her cheeks.

"Ava, stop!" Grant ordered.

She whirled, eyes wide as she watched Grant step into the shower, fully clothed, and pull her into his arms.

"Stop, love," he whispered into her wet hair, stroking her back gently.

Ava sobbed harder, leaning into his warmth, needing the reassurance that he was stronger, badder, meaner, and all those other adjectives that would remind her that Grant was powerful.

"What did he tell you?" he asked, rubbing his hand over her back. She loved the way he touched her. They hadn't been together for long before he'd...well, before. But during that period, she'd loved the way he touched her.

"He said he got turned on when his 'lovers' were scared of him. That he would whip his 'lover' if they weren't scared enough. And he liked to draw blood."

She hid her face against his chest, wishing she'd stayed in her office instead of going down to the ballroom this morning. If she'd been in her office, she could have slammed the door in his face.

But no! She'd had to go down to the ballroom and dream up more ways to make the exhibit better! She'd had to measure spaces that she already knew the measurements of, simply so that she could imagine different colors or draping material in a more appealing way to highlight various artists' works.

"He's gone, love."

Grant said the words, but she couldn't believe him. She believed Willy, the vile bastard.

His arms tightened around her, making her feel secure. "He's gone. I warned him off and he won't bother you again."

Ava pulled back and Grant looked at her arm. The skin was raw and angry, swelling where her nails had dug into the flesh. He ran gentle fingers soothingly over the welts . The itchy, disgusting feeling drifted away wherever he touched her. His fingers were magical, she thought.

"I have a video of Zanika doing something very illegal. Something that would put him away for the rest of his life if the video ever reached the authorities."

She pulled back, staring up at him, unaware of her mouth hanging open until she asked, "Why don't you give it to the police?"

He smiled slightly. "Because Zanika said he'd send his subordinates after me if I ratted on him." He shrugged. "Me keeping the video a secret is a sort of mutually assured destruction, in a way."

"What is on that video?"

Grant pulled her in closer, tucking her head underneath his chin. Ava didn't mind. Not at the moment. She needed this. She needed him.

"I can't tell you, Ava. I can't put you in danger by letting you know what the video shows. Suffice it to say that Willy won't bother you." He sighed, kissing the top of her head. "I should have visited Willy sooner, love. I should have gone directly to him and warned him away from you. I should have done that as soon as I saw you in Houston."

She shifted against him, a surge of power coming over her as she felt his body's reaction to her nakedness. She loved the way he couldn't help but react to her. It made her feel strong. It made her feel beautiful and in control again. Willy's visit was washed away now and she had Grant to thank for it.

"You did it today," she whispered up to him. "Thank you!"

He pulled back again, looking down at her. "Do you believe me? Do you trust me when I say that Zanika won't bother you again?"

"Yes." And that was the absolute truth. She did trust him. She believed in him.

"Good." With that one word, the offering and acceptance of his protection against a force that she didn't know how to fight, she relaxed in his arms.

"Are you done showering?" he asked.

She lifted her head and looked around. "I hadn't realized I was still in the shower," she whispered, then noticed that he was drenched. "You're still dressed!"

"I'm aware of that fact," he growled, pulling her close for a quick brush of his lips against hers before he released her and reached around the glass door for a towel. He handed it to her, then grabbed another. "I hope that you have a dryer."

Ava sighed, feeling...bereft now that he wasn't holding her. The anxiety was seeping back into her thoughts and her skin started crawling again.

Ava wrapped the towel around herself, ignoring her wet hair. It wasn't dripping, so she didn't care. Shivering, she stared at Grant as he tried to dry off from the unexpected shower. "Grant," she whispered, the trembling starting up again.

He turned, his green eyes immediately aware of her fear. "Ava, talk to me." He dropped the towel and moved to her again. "I thought that you understood that I would protect you."

"I do," she acknowledged.

"Then what is it?"

She lifted her eyes, staring into his, and asked, "Would you please... make love to me?" He didn't move, not for a long time. Finally, she shook her head, looking at his chest instead of into his eyes. "It doesn't have to mean anything. It can just be this moment, a stolen moment between us." She blinked, and took in a shuddering breath. "But I understand if you don't–"

She couldn't finish her statement because he kissed her. His strong arms wrapped around her waist, pulling her up onto her toes as he kissed her thoroughly. Ravenously.

"I will make love to you anytime you want," he vowed, his voice thick and husky before he kissed her again.

The towel dropped to the floor and his hands roamed over her naked back, her bottom, her slender waist. She hissed when his hands cupped her breasts and he pulled back, gazing down at his hands as they cupped her curves.

Ava couldn't believe how badly she wanted this. How much she needed this. With every touch, she felt renewed. Cleansed. And so turned on, she couldn't stand still.

She fought his shirt buttons. It was still wet, so it was more difficult than normal, but eventually, she was able to push the shirt out of the way and touch the dark skin underneath. Ava reveled in the sensation of his chest hair tickling her palms. Kissing his chest, she smiled at his growl. Another surge of power shot through her.

"You're killing me, Ava," he whispered, and nipped at her earlobe. A moment later, he lifted her into his arms and carried her off to the bedroom. Carefully, he laid her on the bed, then stepped back and stripped his wet clothes off.

Ava shivered as she watched him. It had been so long since...well, since she'd been interested in intimacy. But there had never been any hesitation when it came to Grant. Not eight years ago and not now.

As he came towards her, big and strong and impressively powerful, she felt that remembered need. He had always been the one.

It was going to hurt when he left again, but she ignored that knowledge. For now, he was here and she needed him. Not just to wipe away the memory of Willy's fingers on her skin, but...but...because she needed him, and that was enough for her at the moment.

"Hey," he whispered against her ear as he slid his body against hers. "Where did you go?"

Ava blinked, then gasped when he cupped her breast. "I'm here," she hissed, arching her back against his touch.

"Tell me to stop if you change your mind."

She smiled up at him, sliding her hands up his shoulders. "I won't. Just...help me forget, Grant. Help me forget and remember."

He hesitated for a moment and Ava had a sudden worry that he might stop. To keep that from happening, she draped her leg over his hip, so that she was touching him in as many places as possible. This, she thought as she closed her eyes, needing to savor the moment, this was what she needed. Grant's touch had changed her life eight years ago. He had given her courage and now she needed him to banish the bad energy left by a creep.

But there was so much more to this than just banishing bad memories and re-living old pleasures. Making love to Grant was like coming alive after years of not realizing she'd been nearly dead. As she rolled so that she was on top, Ava suddenly realized that she'd been barely half alive without him.

"I need more," she explained when she saw the surprise in his eyes as she straddled him.

Then she kissed his chest, exploring every muscle and indentation on his skin. She ran her fingers through the dark hair on his chest, teased his nipples, and smiled when he groaned. Touching her tongue against those nipples, she nipped him just like he'd done so many times to her.

When Grant started to push her onto her back, she sat straighter and shook her head. "No, I need this. Please?" she whispered, knowing that he was strong enough to overpower her if he wanted to take control.

He hesitated for a long moment and Ava stiffened, worried that he wouldn't give this to her. "Please," she whispered, not afraid of pleading.

Finally, Grant relaxed his grip and nodded. "Fine, but I get my turn next," he warned her.

She smiled and even that caused him to hiss.

"Thank you," she said leaning in to place kisses everywhere she could reach. This was it, she thought, even though she couldn't quite define exactly what "it" was.

Kissing lower, she blew lightly on his erection, causing him to groan. Ava felt his hands sift through her hair, not guiding her exactly, but the touch seemed to connect them more deeply as she moved lower still, so that she could kiss and tease his inner thighs. Every so often, she blew on his impressive member, and then went back to kissing the area around it. A lick, a light blow of air, then more kisses. With every lick, she felt his fingers tighten in her hair. She kept teasing, never actually taking him into her mouth. Not yet. She loved this part, teasing Grant and making him burn for her.

If her memory was correct, this was normally the point where he would take control. In the past, Grant would lift her up and roll over so that he was on top.

Sure enough, she soon felt his muscles beginning to clench. To stop him, she took him into her mouth, not giving him any warning. She flicked her tongue against his tip, letting him feel the warmth of her mouth as well as the softness of her tongue as she teased, sliding her mouth up and down over his throbbing shaft, taking as much of him as she could into her mouth.

He hissed and arched his back, showing her that she was doing it right. With her other hand, she stroked the part of him that she couldn't get her lips around, enjoying the way his body was so tightly coiled. She'd done this to him, Ava thought. She'd brought this powerful man to this yearning, desperate need!

"Ava," he groaned, his hands tightening in her hair. She knew what was going to happen and she stopped him by pushing his hands away. She was enjoying herself, enjoying this taste of power. And she wasn't ready to give it up. Not yet, anyway.

"Ava, I'm going to...!" he stopped, his jaw clenching when she tightened her hold and moved her mouth faster over his shaft. No way was she giving this up. Not for anything! She let her breasts brush against his rock hard thigh, watching him fight the pleasure she gave him. He lifted his head, the muscles in his neck straining as he tried to control himself. But it was no use. She flicked her tongue against his shaft, making sure to tease that spot right under the tip where he was most sensitive.

When he groaned, pulling at her hair ever so slightly, she knew that he couldn't hold back any longer and she moved faster.

"Ava!" he yelled, and his climax burst over him, arching against her mouth as he roared with pleasure.

When it was all over, she gave him one more lick, then sat back on her heels, gazing down at him with triumph and...and relief. There was more to it than just those two emotions, but at this moment, Ava was too confused and heartsick to poke at the feelings. She'd do that later. Much later!

"Ava," he sighed, pulling her closer.

Ava snuggled up against his side, enjoying feeling his skin against hers. Remembering the past, thinking about the sad, miserable future that awaited her after he invariably left her again, she couldn't stop the tears from filling her eyes.

Unfortunately one of those betraying tears landed on his chest and he looked up. She tried to hide her face, but he knew. Immediately, they shifted positions, so that she was on the bottom and he covered her.

"Why are you crying?"

Ava bit her lip. "Because I love doing that with you," she said. It wasn't a lie. She truly loved giving him pleasure. But there was more. So much more! He was going to leave her. As soon as this exhibit was over, Grant would head back to Houston, and she'd be alone. Again.

"You're lying," he argued, pressing closer.

Ava laughed weakly, stroking his shoulders, enjoying the way the muscles rippled under her fingers. "I'm not lying. I love feeling powerful like that."

He growled and moved against her, which made her gasp as her nerve endings registered that they were still naked. And her body was still primed and ready.

"Now, it's my turn," he explained in a soft whisper. He stared into her eyes as he said that, and then allowed his green eyes to devour the sight of her breasts, her stomach, and lower. When he brought his eyes back to hers, he smiled. It was a lascivious smile that sent her senses soaring. "Pay back, Ava," he murmured, his hands moving to hers, lifting her arms up over her head. "Pay back."

That's when she knew she was in big trouble.

Sure enough, he started at her neck, teasing the sensitive skin there.

She whimpered at how good he was at finding all of those delicious spots along her neck and shoulders that caused sensations to spark along her skin. Then he moved lower, his mouth capturing one nipple and teasing it until she cried out, begging him to stop. But did he show mercy? Nope! He moved to the other nipple, giving it the same attention. His hand pinned her wrists above her head, not allowing her to move.

It was only when he moved lower still, pressing his body between her thighs that he had to release her hands. By then, Ava was nearly in tears, so turned on and desperate for release, that she nearly pulled him away when he blew on her pink folds. She almost wanted to hate him for the torture he inflicted on her down there. But it was too amazingly beautiful and she lifted her hips, offering herself to him, silently begging him to kiss her there. When his mouth closed over that throbbing nub, Ava couldn't help but arch into his mouth.

He was too good at this! His mouth and lips, oh...and his fingers! Goodness, his fingers were helping to drive her absolutely wild now! Shoving her fingers into his hair, she shifted, trying to show him what her body screamed for.

Wow, he was an excellent student! His mouth moved to the exact spot where she needed him to tease and...!

"Not yet," he warned her, pulling away and grabbing a condom from his still-wet slacks. He rolled the protection down over his shaft, watching her watching him the whole time.

A moment later, he positioned himself above her, poised right at her opening. "You're mine, Ava," he growled, then pressed into her heat, grabbing her hands. Lacing his fingers with hers, he pressed slowly into her, watching her eyes as he filled her body. Slowly at first, he started thrusting, his fingers tightening around hers as she clenched inner muscles around his shaft. "You're *mine*," he said again.

Ava heard his words, but ignored them, turning her head away as his thrusts brought her closer and closer to the release that she needed so desperately. Too soon, her body tightened around his and she felt herself flying with pleasure. It was so intense, she closed her eyes, screaming his name as her hands gripped his.

When she finally opened her eyes, it was to see Grant gazing down at her with a triumphant smirk. At any other time, Ava would have been irritated by his expression. But he'd given her something precious. So, she lifted her limp arms and wound them around his neck, kissing him gently as a silent "Thank you" for such a beautiful experience.

"You okay?" he asked, rolling over so that she was draped across his chest.

"Yes. I'm okay." Better than okay, she thought, putting her cheek to his chest. For a long time, she listened to his heartbeat underneath her cheek while he ran gentle fingers through her hair. It was dry now and probably a tangled mess. But Grant didn't seem to mind.

She fell asleep like that.

Grant knew the exact moment she fell asleep. One moment, he could feel the energy vibrating through her slender, petite body. The next moment, she was completely lax, the tension gone.

He didn't move. For a long time, he simply lay there with her draped across him, reveling in the joy of having her with him again.

Eight years. Eight long years of failing to convince himself that he was fine. That he didn't miss her.

Lies! He'd not been fine. He'd been waiting. For this. For Ava to come back to him. For Ava to realize that they were meant to be together and for her to come to him, tell him that she'd been wrong to kick him out of her life.

Turns out, he was the one rushing back to her. He was the one that was going to have to convince her that they were meant to be together. He would be the one that would have to explain that he wouldn't allow her to kick him to the curb again.

This time, they would work things out, together. They would talk and make plans. He would explain to her *exactly* how things were going to be. He would find a place for them to live, a place large enough for kids. Lots of kids! This house had a decent yard, but not big enough. He wanted...!

Hell, he'd live in a dump if it meant that he would be with Ava. His money, power, and success couldn't even come close to how good he felt right now. All of the success he'd enjoyed in the business world was pathetic compared to this moment. Just holding Ava was worth everything to him.

Chapter 8

The sun shining in her eyes woke Ava the following morning. Sunshine? Blinking, Ava looked around, startled by the bright rays shining through her bedroom window.

"What time is it?" she whispered, looking around for her phone. But it wasn't on the bedside table where she normally put it before falling asleep.

Pushing her hair out of her eyes, she struggled to sit up, wondering why the sheets were tangled around her legs. And where was her pillow? Glancing around, she rolled over, peering over the side of the bed. Sure enough, the pillows were scattered on the floor. That was a bit confusing until she felt the subtle pull in her thigh muscles.

That's when the memories came back.

Last night.

Grant.

The shower and his gentle embrace.

Willy and...no, Willy had gone away. It had been Grant in her arms last night. More specifically, she'd been in his arms. A lot! The man had been ravenous! Every time she'd moved, it seemed to spark more passion in Grant. And he'd been ingenious, some might even say decadent, about sparking that same level of passion within her.

She'd had lovers over the past eight years, but none had ever given her any kind of satisfaction. She'd had sex with them just so that she could look for the same level of joy that Grant had given her all those years ago. But no one else had ever come close. So she'd stopped searching.

Until last night.

Grabbing the pillows, she stuffed two of them behind her back and stared at the empty side of her bed.

"Gone." She whispered that word out loud. He was gone. She had no idea what time he'd left her this morning, or if it had even been morning. When had he left her? And why?

"No!" she whispered to herself, kicking the sheet off. She stomped into the bathroom and flipped on the shower. "I don't care about the why!"

Ava was used to people leaving her. So, this shouldn't be an issue. She should be used to it.

She lathered her hair and scrubbed her body, trying to wash the scent of Grant away. But after lathering her body three times, she gave up. The scent wasn't on her skin. It was in her head. Grant had branded her.

"Damn it!" she muttered, flipping the lever that shut off the water. She grabbed a clean towel and dried off, then stomped into her bedroom. She dressed quickly in a pair of leggings and a tee shirt, pulled her hair up on top of her head and headed downstairs. But when she got to her kitchen, she realized that she wasn't hungry. She should be hungry. After their busy night, she should be ravenous. However, the thought of food made her stomach churn.

She was just about to head back upstairs when she heard the front door open. Her heart stuttered and she grabbed for her cell phone. But it wasn't in the side pocket of her leggings! She hadn't found her cell phone yet!

Who was coming into her house? They had a key, she thought. And then she heard a set of keys fall into the ceramic dish she kept in the front room specifically for that purpose.

"Ava?" Grant's deep, sexy voice called out.

Ava's heart thudded again, but for a different reason now. Still, she forced her silly heart to stop pounding in such a wildly delighted manner. She wasn't happy! He'd still left her this morning!

"I'm in here," she called out, but didn't peek around the door to the kitchen that connected to the front entry hall.

Grant walked into the brightly lit kitchen, holding a bag of bagels and two large cups of coffee. "I'm glad you're finally awake," he said, setting the food down on the white, granite countertops. "I was wondering if you'd ever wake up." He handed her a cup of coffee. "And you don't have *any* food in your house."

She took the coffee, stunned by his words. "Finally?" she chirped.

He focused on peeling the plastic lid off his coffee. "I've been awake for about three hours, waiting for you to wake up."

For some reason, she glanced at her dining room. The table was covered in papers and an open laptop. "You were working?" she asked, turning to look up at him again. Ava was completely confused. Hadn't he left this morning?

"Yes. I had my assistant bring over some contracts I needed to review. I've been on a few conference calls too, but I kept everything low, so you could sleep."

"You...let me sleep?" she asked, her anger evaporating as he explained. He hadn't left her? Those words kept flitting through her mind. She wasn't used to someone sticking around.

"You were exhausted," he replied, leaning in to brush her lips with his. "And you look so beautiful when you're sleeping."

She smiled faintly, charmed against her will.

"I got you a jalapeno and cheddar bagel." He picked up the brown bag and peered inside. "Is that still your favorite?"

"Yes," she replied automatically.

"Good." He pulled out two bagels. One was her jalapeno and cheddar bagel and she recognized the other as an "everything" bagel, which she remembered was his personal favorite.

"So, you'd just left to get breakfast food?" she asked, and mentally cringed at how pathetic she sounded.

"Of course," he replied, then stopped opening cabinets to turn and look at her. "Where did you think I'd gone?"

She shrugged, not sure how to answer his question without revealing more of her personal fears. "Nowhere. I hadn't really thought about it."

He sighed and plopped the bagel down on a cutting board. "You thought I'd make love to you all night, then walk out the front door in the morning without even a word?"

Something like that, she thought to herself, but said, "I didn't know."

He walked over to her and pulled her into his arms. "I'm not leaving you, Ava," he told her, then kissed her lingeringly before releasing her to prep the bagels.

Chapter 9

"Where are we going?" Ava asked two hours later, clicking the seatbelt into place.

"You look beautiful," he said as he started the engine.

"Thank you." She eyed him carefully. "Is that your way of trying to avoid the question? Do you not want me to know?"

He chuckled as he pulled into traffic. "That would be a bit pointless, since you'll find out soon enough." He flipped on his right turn signal and added, "We're going to a wedding."

"Who's wedding?" she asked. "Is it an old friend?"

"The wedding is for an old college friend. I didn't even know he was getting married until a few days ago. He caught me at the end of a business meeting."

"And invited you to his wedding?" She shook her head. "That seems a bit…odd."

He shrugged as he merged onto the highway. "I thought so as well, until I realized that he works for one of the companies I am looking into acquiring."

Ava was silent for a long moment and Grant tightened his grip around the steering wheel. Did she know about his business reputation? Was she aware of how the rest of the world perceived him?

"So, the business is in trouble?" she asked, in a softer tone.

"Yes. It's nearing bankruptcy." He sped up to pass a tractor-trailer. "I don't know if I'm going to buy the business." He took the next exit. "But by going to the wedding, I can speak with his boss, the owner, without anyone knowing that I'm considering the acquisition." He glanced at her. "Is that going to bother you?"

She shook her head, placing a gentle hand on his arm. "Not at all." She sighed and shifted in her seat. "I know what you do. And I appreciate the power that your presence, your interest, has on any business. You've grown your business to a point where, even a hint of your interest means the business is in trouble."

"And you don't think I'm a vulture? Someone who feeds off of the dead?"

Ava turned to look at him more closely and Grant loosened his grip on the steering wheel. His reputation had never bothered him before. He enjoyed his job. He thrived on the challenge of fixing a business and saving it from going under. But some people didn't agree with his methods. Some business people thought he was a scavenger, feeding off the carrion of the business world.

"I think that what you do is brilliant," she said softly. Startled by her words, he glanced at her briefly. There was sincerity glowing in her soft, blue eyes. Her expression, the admiration in her pretty eyes meant…it meant everything to him. Instantly, the tension in his shoulders eased and he focused all of his attention on the road. "I think that you go into a company and save thousands of jobs. Your methods are harsh and, yes, I know that many people get laid off after you come onto the scene. But if you didn't come in to fix the problems, to rejuvenate the business, then *everyone* would be laid off. There are very few people who know how to correct a business that has gone so painfully off course. But you do. I've read the articles about your business acumen, Grant. You've been described as a genius. Harsh and brutal sometimes, but brilliant and creative in redirecting a company that needs an infusion of something more to get them back on track."

There was a long silence. Finally, he said, "Thank you." He hadn't realized how important her opinion was. To him. How much he needed her to understand what and why he did what he did.

"I've often wondered if your interest in the original Halliday Hotel was because it was going under." She toyed with her seatbelt. "Was that why you came into town all those years ago?"

"Yes." He didn't beat around the bush. "Your hotel was in the perfect location," he explained. "It was right off of the highway, out in the woods, but still close enough to the city to make it a prime spot. And being right on the lake like it was?" He chuckled, shaking his head. "It was a gold mine."

She smiled, nodding in agreement. "Yeah, once my father got out of the picture, it was much easier to pick up the pieces and start to make a success of the hotel."

"Jenna has been mentioned in several circles as a potential CEO to replace those in several ailing businesses. Does she know that?"

Ava laughed, shaking her head. "Jenna would never leave Halliday

Hotels. She lives and breathes for the company. She loves every part of her job." She groaned as she said, "I can't tell you how many times I've called her late at night and found she's still at the office."

"That's not good. Everyone needs balance in their lives." He glanced at her as he pulled into the parking lot of a pretty church. "Especially now. You and your siblings should be relaxing now that the success of the business is on track."

She shrugged, slipping out of her seatbelt and reaching for the door handle. "Isn't that how so many of your businesses got off track? By the owners slacking off?"

He chuckled softly, exactly as she'd intended. "You have a point." He parked his beautiful, shiny Lexus right next to a gleaming Ferrari. "Another reason businesses fail is because of overspending by the owners and lack of reinvestment of the company profits back into the business." He glanced pointedly at the cherry red Ferrari.

Ava cringed as they got out, also looking at the impractical car. "It's pretty," Ava commented.

"It's pointless in the city," he countered. "That vehicle can reach speeds of over two hundred miles an hour. It goes from zero to sixty in under four seconds."

Ava looked at him curiously. "How do you know that?"

He took her hand, lacing his fingers through hers. "Because there was a point in my career that I considered buying one."

She leaned her head against his shoulder, then pulled away, remembering that this was only a temporary affair. He would return to his world in Houston eventually. Don't get your heart involved!

"What happened?" she asked, walking beside him towards the wedding venue.

He shrugged slightly, and squeezed her hand. "I reminded myself of my goals."

They entered the church and moved down the aisle towards their seats. She reminded herself firmly that she wasn't going to become involved, but as she sat in one of the church pews, waiting for the ceremony to begin, Ava knew she wanted to learn more about him. Knowledge never hurt anyone, right?

The music sounded, distracting her from her questions. A line of men stepped out from a door at the front of the church, all dressed in dove grey morning suits. It was easy enough to pick out the groom; he was the only one that was pale with nerves.

Ava glanced up at Grant. Would he be nervous on his wedding day? No, she thought with a mental snort. Grant was never nervous. The man was a rock of stability.

With a painful pang, Ava realized she couldn't imagine Grant married. He wasn't just a rock, he was a rock on an island. From what she'd read about him through the years, Grant had dated several women, but none for long. He'd been dubbed the ultimate playboy by more than one magazine.

And that was sad, she thought. Because she suspected Grant could be a wonderful husband and an even better father. He had patience and determination. When he set out to accomplish a goal, he achieved it. Hence, his current level of shocking success in such a short period of time.

Ava smiled, wondering what the groomsmen were talking about. There was a great deal of joking going on. A groomsmen said something to the groom, then the groom would turn and playfully punch his friends' arms.

What a lovely tradition, doing something so magnificent as to promise one's future to another person with one's friends here to witness those vows. The formal attire and the flowers, the music and the fanfare... it all came together to show the seriousness of the promises these two people were about to make. Promises that would alter the path of their lives, as well as the families involved.

Weddings had to be the most amazing evidence that there was still hope in the world.

Grant smothered a groan as the music changed. The congregation waited patiently, watching as the bridesmaids walked slowly down the aisle. He never understood the concept of bridesmaids and groomsmen. Why couldn't two people just head to a justice of the peace and get the deed done? Why all this fanfare? It seemed like a great deal of expense for something that could be done much more efficiently.

Why all the flowers? He understood that they represented fertility. However, surrounding oneself with flowers wouldn't impact the number of children the couple will eventually have in their marriage.

And the music? Was music really necessary to this fiasco? Why not just dive in, say the words, and call it a day? He understood the concept of a nice meal after the vows were exchanged. But why all this fuss and insanity?

The bride came next. The music changed, swelling grandly, and everyone stood up, several people turning to get a better look at the bride. Grant shifted, politely following everyone's gaze, but he wasn't focused on admiring the bride. Instead, he let his gaze skim over the guests, locating the man he needed to speak with after the ceremony. Their eyes connected and the other man nodded, confirming that they would speak later.

That's when Ava sighed and he looked down. She had a dreamy expression on her face, her pretty blue eyes glowing with joy. Was she into all of this wedding stuff? Would she want this kind of a ceremony when they married? And yes, he was more determined than ever to marry Ava now. She was beautiful and passionate, compassionate and intelligent. He wanted all of those emotions directed towards him. He wanted to take care of her, to give her hope in the future, to prove that he was going to stay by her side forever. Till death do us part, he thought.

He didn't bother to look at the bride as she made her way to the alter. He was sure she looked beautiful, but he only had eyes for Ava. He wrapped his arm around her shoulders, pulling her in close.

The music drew to a close and the congregation sat down. Ava leaned her head against his shoulder as he again laced his fingers through hers. "Dearly beloved," the minister began.

Grant didn't hear the rest of the ceremony, too wrapped up in the idea of marrying Ava.

Chapter 10

Ava beamed as she walked into the office on Monday morning, humming a cheerful song as she grabbed a cup of coffee before going to her office.

"Ava?"

Ava turned, looking up to find Felix walking down the hallway towards her.

She smiled up at him, cradling her cup of coffee closer to her heart. "Hey! What are you doing here? I thought you were heading back to Chicago?"

"I am. The company jet is flying me back this afternoon." He shuffled his feet, then rubbed the back of his neck and looked warily up and down the hallway.

"What's on your mind, baby brother?"

His wariness evaporated and Felix rolled his eyes at her. "I'm still several years older than you."

She laughed, delighted with their familiar banter. "Yeah, but you're still the baby brother."

Sighing, he did that up and down the hallway glance again, ramping up Ava's concern. "Talk to me, Felix. You're the guy that hangs off of cliffs! I don't think I've ever seen you nervous until right now."

He checked the hallway a third time.

She snapped her fingers in his face. "Hey! Earth to daredevil! What's going on?"

Felix grumbled. "I'm not a daredevil."

She chuckled. "Felix, something happened to you while you were on the SEAL teams and you need the adrenaline rush to feel truly alive. I get that. It scares the bejeezus out of me and Jenna, probably Pierce too, but we understand." She tilted her head thoughtfully, then added,

"No, actually I *don't* think any of us understand." She moved closer, putting a hand to his arm. "Maybe, you could explain it to us?"

"Explain what?"

"Why you need to put yourself in danger constantly?" she explained. "Why you can't settle down? Why you need to go out into the woods and do dangerous, scary things?"

Felix pressed his lips together, then shuffled his feet again. "Look, I stopped by to speak with you, not for you to question my mental issues."

"Right," she sighed walking into the kitchen and refilling her mug. "So you're here to question my life, but I can't question yours. Is that how this works?"

Felix grinned and Ava suddenly understood why the ladies fell head over heels in love with him. When he smiled, he was devastatingly handsome. Of course, he was pretty good looking even when he wasn't smiling. Obnoxiously tall and overly muscular...okay, she thought about Grant's muscles and how much she loved them. So maybe Felix wasn't overly muscular. He was nicely built, in a bulky sort of way. Pierce, the oldest of all of them was more lithe, but probably just as dangerous.

"Grant Hanover," Felix blurted out, interrupting her contemplation of Grant's muscles.

Ava pulled her attention back to the present and carefully blanked her expression. At least, she hoped it was blank. She seriously hoped that her cheeks didn't look as pink as they felt. "What about Mr. Hanover?" She added some sweetener to her coffee, then picked it up with one hand while shifting her tote back onto her shoulder with the other.

Felix huffed a bit, shifting impatiently on his feet. "Why did you attend a wedding with him over the weekend?"

She blinked, startled by his question. "How in the world did you know that?"

"It was in the news," he pointed out. "There's speculation about you two." He followed when Ava started down the hallway towards her office. "Is the speculation true?"

Ava didn't answer until they were in her office. Unfortunately, as soon as she stepped into her private space, she found Pierce standing by the window, looking grim and determined.

"Pierce?" Ava was so surprised, she had to quickly set her cup of coffee down on the corner of her desk. "What are you doing here?"

Pierce glanced from Felix and Ava, then back again. "You've already asked her?"

Felix nodded sharply. "Yeah, but she hasn't answered yet."

"Answered what?"

Pierce turned to glare at Ava. "Why did you attend a wedding with Grant Hanover this weekend?" he demanded. "After what that man put you through several years ago, he shouldn't be allowed within a hundred miles of you!"

Ava was touched by her oldest brother's vehemence. She glanced over at Felix and her stomach plunged. "Don't!" she told Felix.

"Don't what?" he demanded, crossing his arms over his massive chest.

"Your Navy SEAL training is *not* needed at this time!"

Felix tried to look innocent. He failed! "I don't know what you mean, Ava." But he didn't deny anything.

"Felix," she snapped, exasperated and...yes, touched...by their concern. "I know that you have the skills to do something...horrible...to Grant. And no one would ever find his body. But I'm asking you to not hurt him."

Pierce stepped forward. "Then tell us why you were with him this weekend."

Ava lifted a hand, dumping her tote bag beside her desk. "He has no interest in taking over Halliday Hotels, Pierce."

"I don't give a damn about his business concerns!" Pierce growled and Ava suddenly understood why Pierce was a terror in the business world. She'd never seen this side of him, but she had to admit that it was impressive! "Why is he here? I won't let him hurt you again!"

"I won't either," Felix inserted, puffing up his chest.

Ava glanced between her brothers. They were both shockingly intimidating. And it was incredibly sweet of them to be so...brotherly...about her relationship with Grant. "Look guys, it's nothing. He can't hurt me, because I'm not going to become emotionally involved with him this time. And the wedding was merely a business issue. He wanted to speak with another business owner, but didn't want the press to find out. The wedding was a perfect cover for him to talk without anyone becoming suspicious." She looked at her brothers again, hoping that they understood what she was saying. "He left immediately after the wedding, flying to the company's locations to do a walk through of the factory buildings with the owners." She lifted her hands, palms out defensively. "I promise, me being at the wedding with Grant wasn't significant." She didn't mention that Grant had spent the night with her the night before, or that he was protecting her from a criminal that threatened to do horrible things to her. Nope, that information was on a need-to-know basis, and her overly protective and surprisingly dangerous brothers didn't need to know.

Ava smiled at them, and pulled a marketing booklet out of her tote bag. "I have a meeting in," she checked her watch, "five minutes. I still need to finish preparing."

Her brothers looked unconvinced, but Ava smiled gently at both of them. "I promise, I'm okay. Grant won't hurt me. Burned once, shame on you. Burned twice, shame on me," she quipped, wrinkling her nose. "I won't be burned twice. I learned my lesson the first time."

When her brothers left, Ava took a moment to smile with real warmth. Her brothers hadn't ever gone all brotherly on her before. It was... sweet!

Still, she had to get going if she was going to make it to the meeting. Tucking the pamphlet under her arm, she headed for the marketing conference room. As soon as this meeting was over, Ava planned on spending the rest of the afternoon working on the art exhibit. She needed to finalize the details and have a meeting with the artists.

Willy stalked into his office, snapping his fingers at his assistant.

"What can I do for you?" the pretty blonde asked, lifting her pen, letting it hover over a notebook. Today, she wore a tight, pink sweater with a pair of jeans that she'd probably painted on this morning. She also tottered about in a pair of heels so high, a light wind could knock her over.

"What's on the agenda for today?" he demanded, throwing himself into the leather chair behind his desk. He'd stolen the desk out of an old duke's house several years ago. Willy had gotten rid of the old man for his son, albeit for a hefty price tag. The desk had been Willy's "tip" for a job well done.

"Ummm..." the blond woman, Desiree, blinked owlishly. "I don't have anything scheduled for you today, sir." She shifted on her feet, blinking her overly done eye lashes as she waited for instructions.

Willy thought about smacking her...but no. It took too much energy. Besides, his assistant wasn't the woman he wanted to smack around .

A dark haired, blue eyed goddess popped into his head. Yes, he'd definitely enjoy smacking Ava Halliday around. But the bitch had gotten a "protector"! And one with a hell of a good reason to stay the hell away from her.

Damn Grant Hanover! Willy had messed up all those years ago and Hanover, the shrewd bastard, had enough evidence that...dammit! If only the bastard had come around the corner five minutes later. Or even better, if the ass hadn't been looking into that factory down by the harbor as a potential business investment. Why did the man have to go after the bad businesses? It didn't make any sense to Willy – except that Hanover was one of the richest bastards around these days, so he must be onto something.

"Would you like some coffee, sir?" Desiree asked.

Damn, the woman was an idiot! "Yes!"

"With cream and sugar, like always?" she asked, tilting her head slightly as if Willy's answer was supremely important.

Willy barely restrained himself from rolling his eyes. The woman couldn't help the fact that she was stupid. Hell, he'd hired her specifically for that attribute. No sense having a smart bitch around the office. Anyone with even the smallest hint of intelligence would understand how Willy made his living and might go to the police. He killed enough people, sometimes just for sport and sometimes for profit.

Thinking of lovely women, Willy surveyed the woman's ass as she bent over. Why was she wearing jeans? He'd specifically told her to wear dresses! Although, ever since discovering the blue eyed Halliday bitch, Willy hadn't been tempted by any other woman. What was it about Ava Halliday that made his body twitch with interest while other women, the easy, dim-witted women that he used to prefer, left him feeling...limp and lifeless.

He glanced down at his willy, mentally commanding the stupid organ to stand at attention. Nothing. He glanced over at Desiree's pert ass, then down at his crotch. Still nothing!

For a moment, he worried maybe he'd lost it! So, he rubbed himself through his slacks. Immediately, his pecker started to come alive. Whew! Thank the saints! Still, it took effort, so he abandoned his rubbing just as his assistant turned to bring his coffee to him. No use letting Desiree know what it took to get himself up these days! She'd laugh at him and no one, absolutely no one, laughed at Willy!

"Here you go, sir," Desiree sing-songed, placing the cup of coffee in front of him with a flourish. "Would you like me to call the barber shop to see if Tommy and Angelo are chatting with Milton?"

Willy contemplated a bit more rubbing, wanting to reassure himself that he was still a fully functioning man. But with Desiree's big...he didn't know what color eyes she had...staring at him, he didn't want to embarrass himself. In the past, he would have ordered his assistant to bend over and let him go at her from behind whenever the mood struck him. So, why wasn't he interested in Desiree?

It was her, he thought. Desiree was too...something. He'd have to fire her ass and get someone in that appealed to his pecker more. He'd keep Desiree around long enough to find someone else though. He didn't want Manny coming around and finding the front office empty. That wouldn't look good. In his business, perception was everything. The perception of efficiency, of power, of control. And a beautiful woman sitting in the front office was a sign of power. Plus, every one of his colleagues who came through for a chat assumed that he was banging whatever bimbo was guarding his office.

He was just about to get up and head out again, when his cell phone rang. "Yeah?"

"Hey, Willy!" Willy grinned when he recognized his friend Milo. Willy relaxed and leaned back in his faux-leather chair, propping his feet up on the desk. "How's it hanging?"

Willy forced a laugh, but glared down at his crotch, unwilling to admit that his pecker was hanging a bit too limply lately. "A little to the right," he joked. "How ya doin' Milo?"

"Can't complain!"

"What's up? I know you didn't call to shoot the breeze. You always have an agenda." He shifted in the chair, getting more comfortable now that one of the guys he worked with was calling him. That was significant. Power. The perception of power!

"I heard something about an art exhibit happening at one of those fancy-ass hotels downtown. Word on the street is that you got something going with it. That true?"

Willy's feet dropped off of the desk with a thud. He rallied quickly. "Eh, I was looking into it, but I had to toss the idea."

"Why the hell would you do that? I got a bunch of paintings I can add to the exhibit. We need that money cleaned, Willy. How much have you cleaned so far?"

Willy didn't want to admit that he'd managed less than ten percent of the laundering so far. He rubbed the bridge of his nose. "Yeah, well, that art exhibit...too much security."

Milo snorted. "Like that's ever been a problem for you!" He laughed heartily. "Seriously, we need that money cleaned and out, soon. Why don't you come by later today, when you're not busy, and take a look at these paintings I found. If you can get them into that exhibit, I guarantee that I'll have the buyers lined up. I got a bit of cash that needs to be filtered too. It's a win for both of us."

Willy thought of the video. Grant Hanover had threatened him with the video but...hell, why hadn't he already turned that video in to the police?

Sitting up, he bit his lip, considering the possibilities. Why the hell hadn't Hanover already turned him in? That video would put Willy away for life!

Making a snap decision, he nodded his head, chuckling to himself. "Yeah! Yeah, Milo, why don't I come by a bit later this afternoon. Lemme see if I can shuffle a few appointments around. Maybe after lunch?"

Milo laughed. "Absolutely! Let's meet at the diner on First Avenue. My niece just started waitressing there and we can give her a big tip."

"Always happy to help out the family," Willy replied. "I'll see ya at lunch." And he ended the call, leaning back in his chair again.

"Something going on, Willy?" Desiree asked, walking into the office to look out the window. She flipped the blinds open a bit, then backed away. Why did she keep on doing that? Eh, the bitch left his office whenever he got on the phone, giving him the privacy that he needed. That was what was important. What did he care if she wanted to peek out through the window every so often? Her office was a tomb. No windows at all. She just stared down the long hallway at the elevators. But since there weren't any other tenants in this building...well, no *actual* tenants, he corrected...there weren't even any visitors coming or going off of the elevators. The building was empty except for his office, unless one wanted to look at the books. This building cleaned about fifty-thousand dollars in cash every month from the "tenants" who theoretically paid their rent.

"Of course there's something going on," he snarled at the idiot woman. "I always have something going on!"

The woman held up her hands, palms out as she walked back out of his office. "Sorreee!" she grumbled and pulled his door closed.

"Stupid bitch," he snapped, then took a long sip of the sweet coffee while rubbing his crotch. Nothing! "Oh hell no!" He glared down at his groin. His limp organ mocked him through the polyester pants!

Standing up, he took a long swallow. Maybe he should switch to decaf? No, caffeine wasn't the issue. It was just that he wanted Ava. Yeah, that was it. And no one else would work for him. Willy had no idea why his prick had become so picky, but that must be it. No way would he accept that he was impotent! He'd head over to Ava's place and get a good look at her in those colorful outfits she liked to wear. Yes, that would get him up and going! Maybe he could even pull her into a coat closet and have a bit of fun!

Ava tapped her pen as she contemplated the layout of the various paintings. She had three hundred paintings that would start arriving in three days. As soon as the business conference was finished, she could start setting up for the exhibit, so she needed to have everything figured out by then.

"Ava, my lovely lady!" a sniveling voice called out.

Ava spun around, her eyes widening as she watched Willy Zanika sauntering towards her wearing a tacky white suit with a maroon dress shirt underneath. A white suit? Did the man have to announce to everyone that he was an organized crime boss?

"Get away from me!" she hissed, backing away.

"Now is that any way to treat your best friend?" he taunted, dropping his arms so that his hands covered his heart. "I'm wounded, my dear." He moved closer, bending over to whisper into her ear. "Especially since we need to discuss how we're going to clean all that money!" He straightened up and smiled down at her. "Oh, and did I mention that my friend has about fifty more paintings that you're going to include in the exhibit? That will help with my job," he whispered.

"I'm not laundering for you!" she hissed back, then looked around to make sure no one had heard her. She didn't want anything tarnishing this exhibit!

"Of course you are, my dear." And then he laughed and turned away. "I'll send the pictures over, darlin'! Put them in the center where more people can see 'em!"

And then he was gone.

Ava stared at the place where the slimy, lower-than-a-human had been standing, revulsion washing over her. She hated that man. But at least he hadn't touched her this time. Nor had he made any more disgusting threats.

Still, she needed to tell Grant. She couldn't allow Willy to threaten her. If Grant couldn't stop the slimy man from using her exhibit, then she'd go to the police. Okay, so she'd go to Pierce first, then she'd go to the police. She wasn't afraid of her brother anymore. She was sick of being afraid!

Chapter 11

"Does Mr. Hanover have five minutes to spare?" Ava asked, her fingers clenching around the strap of her tote bag. It had been three days since she'd seen Grant. And it had been four days since the night they'd spent together. Four long, lonely nights in which she'd struggled to sleep because she'd missed his touch so much. After just one night in his arms, she was addicted.

The man sitting behind the desk looked up from his computer and blinked at her. "Five minutes?" He immediately started shaking his head. "I'm sorry, but Mr. Hanover is booked solid for the next twelve hours. May I make an appointment for you?" he asked and clicked on his computer, pulling up Grant's calendar. "What's the nature of the issue you need to discuss with Mr. Hanover?"

"It's personal," a male voice announced from behind Ava.

A split second later, Grant wrapped an arm around her waist. He didn't hesitate as he pulled her into his arms and kissed her. Because there was an audience, he thankfully kept the caress brief, but the heat in his eyes warned her that the small kiss wasn't enough for him.

Keep your cool, Ava reminded herself, even as she sighed with something akin to joy as she leaned against his chest.

"This is Ava Halliday," he told his assistant. "If she calls or stops by the office, please interrupt me, no matter what I'm doing."

"Yes, sir," the man replied, adding a sharp nod for emphasis.

"This way," Grant said, guiding her through a set of double doors into his office. When the doors closed firmly behind them, Ava's heartbeat increased. "You look so hot," he growled, his hands slipping underneath the knit, blue shirt that matched the flowing, silk skirt she'd chosen this morning. "The color makes your eyes seem incandescent."

She tilted her head and Grant took advantage of the angle by nibbling on the newly exposed skin. "Is that a good thing?"

He nipped at her earlobe, causing her to jump in reaction.

"Very good," he growled, his hands on her waist, pulling her closer. Ava stepped backwards, but she didn't move fast enough so he lifted her into his arms and placed her on his desk. "There," he replied, looking down at her. "You look so prim and proper at the moment."

Ava laughed, delighted with his teasing. It brought back so many memories of their time together. But she hadn't realized that Grant was still capable of that kind of teasing. "I *am* prim and absolutely proper," she lied. Well, sort of lied. She was always prim and proper, except when Grant was around. He brought out the not-so-proper aspect of her personality. And the way his fingers were sliding up her leg, creeping underneath the hem of her silk skirt was highly improper.

She gasped and grabbed at his wrist, but her grip didn't slow him down. "I don't think you're improper enough," he explained, watching her eyes as his hand crept higher and higher, his fingers sending lightning to that sensitive spot at the apex of her thighs. "I think you should show me just how non-prim you can be."

He leaned forward, brushing his lips against hers temptingly. Ava kissed him, moaning when his tongue invaded her mouth, demanding a response. "Have I mentioned how beautiful you are?" he asked. His hand moved from her thigh to her hair, tilting her head so that he could deepen the kiss. Ava shifted closer so she could get more of that kiss, needing him to...to what? She grabbed his tie, pulling herself closer still, wrapping her legs around his waist before grabbing his shoulders.

His groan thrilled her and she might have smiled, but Ava couldn't be sure. Everything was a haze of desire, except for the fact that he was still wearing too many clothes. Her fingers moved from his neck, sliding down over his chest, exploring every angle they encountered. She didn't stop until her fingers brushed over the throbbing erection pressing insistently against his dress slacks.

"Ava!" he groaned, then jerked her closer still with his hands under her bottom, angling her so that she was perfectly aligned with him. She gasped, her head spinning with the new, delightful pressure. She couldn't stop her hips from rolling, pressing against him, desperate for the release she knew he could give her!

She fumbled blindly for the zipper, then pushed the material aside until...yes! His shaft was in her hands, her fingers exploring. But he was doing the same thing. She heard something rip but couldn't make sense of the sound. Mostly because his long finger penetrated her body, sliding through the folds before coming out again, flicking against that nub. Ava gasped, remained very still for a moment, then wiggled closer.

"Yes!" she whispered against his mouth as he kissed her and flicked that nub while she stroked him, their hands moving in the same rhythm.

"Don't stop!" he urged, then moved his hand faster. Ava understood and stroked him faster as well.

Abruptly, Grant pulled away and grabbed a condom, tearing the package open and quickly sheathing himself. It took only seconds, but Ava was impatient for him. So when he pulled her to the edge of his desk, she leaned back, eager for him. When he thrust into her, she gasped as he filled her completely, then receded. Whimpering, she pushed back up and grabbed his shoulders, using the leverage to shift against him. Finally, they found their rhythm, oblivious of the rest of the world. The only sounds were their gasps of pleasure as their bodies strained towards that cliff. When it came, Grant covered her cries with his mouth, absorbing her pleasure even as he found his own release.

Ava's arms trembled as she held onto him, her body coming back to the present as her mind slowly started working again.

Smiling up at Grant, she wanted to laugh. Biting her lower lip, she let her fingers slide into his hair at the base of his neck. "Hello," she whispered.

His green eyes opened wide, then he threw back his head, laughing. Then he lowered his head to kiss her briefly before he slowly pulled out of her. He grabbed several tissues from behind his desk to clean up with. "I'll be right back," he told her, pausing to drop another kiss on her lips before he disappeared into a hidden bathroom. When he emerged again, Ava had already straightened her clothing as much as possible and found her panties, which were torn from his urgency. She smiled, stuffing the material into her purse as she turned to face him.

Immediately, he wrapped his arms around her, pulling her against his chest. "How are you doing?"

That's when she remembered Willy Zanika's visit earlier today. "I still need your help," she told him.

"Anything. What's up?"

He kept his arm around her waist and Ava didn't mind. She enjoyed the fact that he liked touching her. It seemed as if she'd gone her whole lifetime wishing for some small scrap of human affection. So if Grant was willing to give her that, she was going to enjoy it for as long as this...whatever it was, lasted.

"Willy came to visit me again this morning." Because she was still in his arms, she felt his muscles tighten.

"The bastard!" Grant hissed. "He doesn't understand the peril he's put himself into!"

"I got the impression that he doesn't think you are much of a threat."

Grant pulled away and stalked over to his computer. He typed something in and his calendar popped up. Grabbing the phone, he dialed his assistant. "Brad, cancel my next three meetings this afternoon. I have something I need to take care of."

Ava's eyes went wide as she stared up at Grant. "What are you going to do?"

He took her hand and kissed her fingertips before he said, "I need you to go back to your office and stay there. In fact, check into a hotel room and don't go home tonight. Can you do that for me?"

Ava's heart lurched. "Yes. But I need you to tell me what's going on."

He shook his head. "It's better if you don't know." He paused, his hands resting on her hips. "Do you trust me?"

Ava swallowed hard, too overwhelmed to form words so she nodded her head.

"Good. Then I need you to do exactly what I said. I'll be fine. I promise. But before I can do *anything*, I need to know that you're safe. Will you text me when you reach your office? Even better, can you work from a hotel room this afternoon? Under an assumed name?"

"Yes, of course," she replied, frantically thinking through the details. She'd have to grab her laptop and her contracts. She'd cancel her afternoon appointments and...and she'd log into the system from her office and check into a room. Yes, she could do all of that.

"Good. One more thing," he said, pausing to lock his laptop again before he tucked it under his arm. "Give me a word, something that only you and I know about."

She considered for a moment. "Orange," she whispered, her terror ramping up. "Is that going to be necessary?"

He shook his head and kissed her again. "I don't know, but I refuse to take chances with your safety." He took her hand and led her out of his office. They rode down the elevator in silence, as Ava clenched his hand tightly, terrified of what might happen next.

When they reached the parking garage, he walked her to her car and stood beside it as she got in. "Remember," he said, bending down to her level, "text me as soon as you get to the hotel room."

She hesitated for a moment. "Are you...will you be okay? Are you going to be safe, Grant?"

"Absolutely," he assured her without any hesitation. "I'm perfectly safe." He stood up and closed the door, then watched until she drove away before he went to his own car. Ava watched him in the rearview mirror until he ducked into a vehicle. This one wasn't his normal, sleek Lexus. She didn't recognize this car and noticed that it was a nondescript vehicle. One that would blend in with thousands of other cars on the road.

For some reason, that knowledge calmed her a tiny bit. Not a lot. She was still terrified for him. And for herself, but she would be safely locked up in a hotel room. Grant was the one putting himself in danger. For her!

As soon as that thought hit her, Ava knew that she was lost. Her efforts to keep her emotions in check during their brief fling were pointless. She was in love with Grant. Again. Madly, wildly in love with him.

Was that just because her body was thrumming from yet another lovely moment in his arms? She blushed, thinking of how they'd had sex on his desk. Good grief, his assistant had only been a wall away! Had he heard them? She certainly hoped not.

That brought her back to the danger Grant was heading into, to protect her. She didn't want him to do that. Not for her! She'd...Ava decided to just let Willy take control of the exhibit. Or maybe she should just cancel it entirely. She could blame the cancelation on...on a wedding? Yes, maybe that could work.

Five minutes later, she pulled into the underground parking garage for the hotel and parked in a visitor's space. She didn't want to park in her assigned space, not wanting anyone to know that she was here. Parking her car here was a bit more anonymous, she told herself as she flung her tote bag over her shoulder. She'd head into her office and reserve a room for herself. Not a suite, she decided. No, she'd get a regular hotel room. They were nice enough, with a small sitting area and a table where she could work.

Ava snorted as she walked into her office, sat down at her desk, and logged into the reservation system. It took only a few moments to get a key card, then she grabbed her laptop and some papers, told her assistant that she'd be out for the rest of the day, then headed to the room she'd assigned herself.

Once she was behind locked doors, she pulled out her cell phone and texted Grant. "*I'm in a room.*"

"*Good. Stay there until you hear from me.*"

"*Be safe!*" she texted back.

"*Will do.*"

Ava pulled open her laptop and the contracts she needed to review. But she couldn't concentrate. Her hands were shaking and her mind skittered away whenever she tried to focus on the text on the contracts.

Finally, she stopped trying and stood up, gazing out the window as she wondered what Grant was doing.

Chapter 12

Grant stepped into the elegant office, noting the security systems in place, as well as the guards stationed at the office door.

"Is Mr. Matero available?"

The pretty woman with the low cut dress and lots of bleach blond hair glanced up from her computer. This wasn't the ignorant-bimbo type of receptionist. The sharp, assessing glance she gave Grant warned him that this woman was capable of much more than making coffee.

The woman picked up the phone, then held it a few inches from her ear. "May I tell him your name?"

"Grant Hanover," he explained. "I need to speak to him regarding Willy Zanika."

The woman's eyes widened and she hesitated for a long moment, but then she nodded slightly and dialed a number. "Mr. Grant Hanover is here to speak with you, sir. He says he need to discuss Mr. Zanika."

There was a bit of mumbling on the phone, then the woman nodded and hung up. "Mr. Matero will see you immediately."

"Thank you," he said, nodding politely to her before he turned and headed to the double doors. There was a slight buzzing sound before he pushed through the doorway. Obviously, Mr. Matero had excellent security.

"Mr. Hanover!" the amiable man with a handlebar mustache exclaimed, coming around a large desk as he buttoned his suit jacket. "It's a pleasure to meet you. Your reputation precedes you."

Grant shook the man's hand, nodding to him. "As does yours."

Mr. Benny Matero gestured to a small sitting area. "Please. Sit. Would you like some coffee?"

"That would be nice. Thank you," Grant replied, even though he didn't particularly want coffee.

The blond woman strode into the office, already carrying a tray with two cups of coffee as well as cream and sugar, setting the tray down on the low coffee table before walking out of the office, pulling the door closed behind her.

"Please, help yourself."

Grant took one of the cups of coffee and pretended to sip it. He didn't drink it, aware that this man was a criminal to his core. Grant didn't trust him not to have the coffee poisoned in some way.

"Mr. Matero, I'd like–"

"Please, call me Benny. And I will call you Grant." He lifted his hands outward, balancing the coffee with one hand. "We are friends, correct?"

Grant tilted his head slightly, neither denying nor confirming their relationship. "Benny," he started again, "I knew Willy Zanika years ago. A little over eight and a half years, to be precise."

"Ah, I'm sorry."

Grant chuckled, liking the man already. "Thank you." He placed the laptop on the table. "I filmed Willy doing something that the police would be very interested in seeing."

"Why have you brought this to me instead of the police?"

Grant's eyes sharpened on the other man. "For two reasons. First, the video involves a pretty major predator in an older neighborhood of Seattle. And I made an agreement with Willy."

"What is the nature of your agreement?"

"He leaves me and my family alone and I don't go to the police."

Benny's gaze sharpened. "And how has he violated this agreement?"

"He threatened my fiancée." He paused to let that sink in before he continued. "I warned him a few days ago, but Willy decided to ignore it."

"What happened?" Benny demanded, his eyes turning cold, his body very still. He was angry. Good! Grant was counting on that.

"After warning him away from her, he approached her again with the same threat. I warned him to stay away and he ignored the warning. Now I'm here to ask you if you'd prefer to handle this issue or if you'd prefer for me to go to the police. Whichever is in your best interest."

Benny didn't move for a long moment, nor did Grant. Benny Matero was a good businessman who had a reputation for always fulfilling his promises. Those promises might be one of evil intentions or a vow of protection. Either way, he always followed through. And if someone violated his word, Benny never allowed the violation to go unpunished.

"Please, continue," Benny said, nodding encouragingly.

Grant flipped open the laptop and pressed the button to start the video. "I filmed this several years ago when I was considering buying a warehouse down by the waterfront." He stopped talking and let the video speak for itself. The images were captured on a cell phone and clearly showed Willy confronting someone who had their hands up, obviously showing that he didn't have a weapon. Willy was pointing the gun at the other man. Grant had been too far away to be able to record the audio, but in this instance, words were not necessary. There was an argument, Willy laughed, the man pleaded, dropping down on his knees. Willy laughed again, then lifted the pistol and shot the man in the head. There was still silence from Benny Matero as Willy kicked the body into the river, stuffed the pistol into the back of his pants, then sauntered away as if nothing of consequence had just occurred.

The video continued, filming Willy getting into his car and driving away. The license plate on the car was clear in the video.

When it ended, Grant closed the laptop and waited.

"You have excellent evidence against one of my foot soldiers, Mr. Hanover."

"I have this file saved in various places around the world, with instructions that the video be released on the event of my death." He paused, letting that sink in. "However, if you would like to take care of this issue, then I will no longer need the video."

Benny Matero's eyes sharpened on Grant. The man thought for a moment, and nodded his head. "I will deal with this issue, Mr. Hanover."

Grant stood up and extended his hand. "Thank you. I understand that your word is worth something, so I will consider this issue closed."

Benny stood as well, shaking Grant's hand. "I appreciate your trust in me, Mr. Hanover."

Grant left the office, staring straight ahead. He was eager to get back to Ava and ensure that she was safe. He didn't want her in any more danger! She'd endured enough!

Willy stared at the text message as sweat immediately started forming on his face. "What the hell?" he muttered. The man hadn't contacted him in...well, ever! Willy prided himself on having a reputation as a bad-ass. But Matero was on a whole other level of scary!

So, why the hell did Matero want to speak with him?

Being called to the big boss's office was...it had to be bad! Very bad!

He looked around, but the old warehouse was abandoned. It was where he stored the cash that needed to be laundered.

Was that it? Was Matero worried about the laundering schedule? Willy was a bit behind, but that was why he'd pressed that blue-eyed chick again. He needed to get that money cleaned!

Wiping the sweat from his brow, he sighed and stomped his feet, impatient now. Maybe he should swing by and chat with Ava Halliday, get some numbers together. He would explain how many paintings he was bringing to the exhibit. He'd find out how many other paintings from the local artists she would supply. Then he could do the calculations to determine how much money he could push through the exhibit.

Yeah, that was a good idea. He'd stop by her office and get more information. Matero was a businessman. He didn't care *how* things were done, he just expected results.

Taking one last glance at the storage bins where the cash was hidden, he headed out to his car.

The phone ringing made Ava jump. Pressing a hand to her pounding heart, she stared at her cell phone. Was it Grant? Was he finished with whatever he'd been doing? Ava grabbed her phone, but the number wasn't Grant's.

For a long moment, her finger hesitated over the button that would answer the call. Should she?

In the end, she worried that Grant was hurt and someone was calling her to get him help.

"Yes?" she answered warily.

"Ava!" a creepily familiar voice answered. "You wound me by not being where I need you to be," Willy said with his nasally, sniveling voice.

Ava gripped the phone more tightly. "What do you want, Willy?"

Willy laughed. "You know it's always been you, love. I've always wanted you!" He chuckled again, but the sound was flat and ugly. "I've wanted you on your back, letting me have my way with you. Or on your knees, doing whatever the hell I want you to do with that pretty mouth of yours."

Ava closed her eyes in revulsion. "Stop it!" she snapped.

He laughed again, then dropped the bomb. "Well, since you aren't where you are supposed to be, perhaps I'll just run a knife between your boyfriend's ribs." He made a noise, making Ava think that Willy already had Grant tied up somewhere. "Do you think I'm skilled enough to miss his lungs?" he asked, a sound in the background coming through.

Ava swallowed painfully, tears forming immediately. She couldn't handle the thought of Grant getting hurt. "Don't you *dare* hurt him!" she hissed.

"Ah, but here's the rub," he replied. "You've sicced your boy on me and now I need to move faster. I dislike being thwarted, especially by a woman I'd like to bed." He laughed at his joke. "Now be a good girl and meet me downstairs in your beautiful hotel's lobby so that we can discuss the details, eh?"

Ava closed her eyes and tried to sound confident as she asked, "When?"

"Now, my lovely woman!" He practically snarled the words. "Get down here now, or I'll cut him into little bits!"

The call ended. Ava chewed her lower lip and tried to think. She should have asked Willy to give the secret code word she'd given to Grant earlier today, just to confirm that Willy actually had Grant. But since she hadn't, and there was no way she was going to call him back, Ava didn't know what to do next.

So, she found someone who would.

She hurried down the hallway, using the employee service areas to get to the next building over where the executive offices were located. Ava ignored the startled expressions on the other employees' faces when she ran by, kicking off her heels when they slowed her down.

It wasn't until she burst into Felix's office that she stopped, gasping for breath. "I need your help!"

Felix stared at Ava for a long moment. But just a moment. Felix was a former Navy SEAL, after all. He was used to surprises and reacting quickly. He morphed into warrior mode instantly. "What's happening?" he demanded, coming around his desk.

"I've been seeing Grant Hanover again," she started off, her eyes wide with barely controlled fear.

"We know that. What's wrong?"

"We?" she questioned, then turned, noticing that Pierce and Jenna were also in the office. For an instant, she felt the stab of pain that her siblings were having a meeting without her, but she pushed it aside. Right now, she needed to save Grant.

Closing her eyes, she shook her head, and organized her thoughts. "Two weeks ago, a man named Willy Zanika came to me about the art exhibit that I'm organizing. He said that he wanted to launder money through the exhibit. He told me that he'd handle the transactions. I knew that he was going to swindle the artists, as well as bring in a bad element to the hotel, so I flew to Houston and asked Grant to help me get rid of him. I knew Grant had some type of relationship with Willy and that maybe he could talk to Willy and get him to leave me alone. Apparently, Grant has some sort of hold over Willy and now Willy has Grant captive and is threatening to hurt him if I don't come down to the lobby to speak with him."

Ava took a breath, praying that Felix understood and wouldn't waste time asking questions.

Thankfully, Felix was able to fill in enough of the details on his own.

His dark eyebrows were low over his blue eyes, making him appear almost sinister. "Right." He turned to Jenna. "In five minutes, go down to the lobby with Ava. Stand by the left entrance door so that the bar is to your back."

Ava opened her mouth to ask why, but Jenna nodded sharply and grabbed Ava's wrist, pulling her out of Felix's office. Ava heard Felix give instructions to Pierce. Because Ava was looking over her shoulder as Jenna tugged her along, Ava saw Pierce heading to the employee entrance elevator on the opposite end of the hallway. Pierce looked just as fierce and terrifying as Felix, who slipped out of his office as well, tossing his tie onto someone's desk and unbuttoning the cuffs of his dress shirt as he went.

Felix didn't head for the elevators. Instead, Ava saw him going towards the stairs. She didn't understand, but since she'd gone to Felix, she needed to trust him.

The doors to the elevator closed and she held her breath. She prayed Felix called security for back up. But maybe he hadn't. Most of the security team were dressed to be obvious, their presence used as a deterrent as well as an investigative staff.

"You're worried," Jenna commented softly as they watched the numbers above the door indicate the floors they were passing.

"I am."

"Do you love him?"

Ava hesitated and sighed, her shoulders slumping slightly. "Yes."

"Even after what happened eight years ago?"

Ava's startled glance looked at her older sister. "How did you know about eight years ago?"

Jenna sighed and pulled her eyes away from the numbers, looking directly into Ava's gaze. "Because you were madly in love with Grant eight years ago. We all knew it." She looked back up at the numbers. "We tried to comfort you after he left, but you retreated into your art and the marketing efforts." She was silent for a long moment, and then she added, "That was when I accepted that I'd lost you as a sister."

Ava's eyes burned with sudden tears. "You're still my sister!" she said fiercely, wishing that was true.

"No, you were so sad after that. You rejected us. We couldn't break through the wall that you put up around yourself." She looked at Ava with empathy in her eyes. "I understand. You were trying to protect yourself. So many people had left you already. You were reeling. But..." she lifted a hand and wiped a tear from her cheek. "But I missed you."

Before Ava could respond, the elevator doors opened. "I'm going to walk to the left of you. Just be ready."

Ready? Ready for what? Ava followed her sister's instructions. Immediately, she noticed Willy Zanika standing in the middle of the lobby. His knowing smirk spoke of his confidence and Ava wanted to scratch the bastard's eyes out! She wanted to yell at him, to demand that he release Grant. She was here. She'd do whatever he asked of her as long as Grant was safe.

She walked up and glared at him, her anger and revulsion evident in her eyes. "Where is Grant?"

He snorted. "Your boyfriend is safe enough," he told her. Then he grabbed her upper arm. "But you're coming with me. We have some final details to work out before I visit my boss."

Ava wanted to jerk her arm from his grip, but she was painfully aware that Grant wasn't in sight. He hadn't called her and...where was her phone? Ava realized she'd forgotten her cell phone in her room.

Oh, good grief! She'd been so frantic to save Grant that she hadn't remembered to take her phone with her when she'd run to her brother's office!

That's when she remembered Felix's instructions. Go to the bar's entrance. She glanced over her shoulder at the entryway to the bar. There wasn't anything there. It was completely empty!

Still, she angled her body in that direction.

"Where the hell are you going?" Willy hissed at her.

Ava frowned up at him, digging in her heels to keep him from bodily moving her. She added a few innocent blinks, trying to look sincere. "I thought you were trying to leave the hotel?"

"I am!" he snapped and jerked on her arm. "This way!"

She pulled back, ignoring the bruises she could tell were forming on her arm. "The parking garage is this way," she argued, pointing towards the bar. "If we go through those doors, the security will stop me because of my badge."

He leaned into her, his face barely an inch from hers. "What the hell are you trying to pull?"

Ava fought to not cringe as his hot, stinking breath washed over her face. "That door is for guests, Willy," she explained with what she hoped was a look of innocence. "If I go through that door, the security office and everyone in the personnel office will be alerted. I'll be stopped by every security guard on duty. Employees are not allowed to go through the main entrance." She pointed towards a doorway off to the side of the bar. "Besides, that door leads directly to the parking garage. We put that door there specifically so that we could entice the people who work close by, so that they don't need to go all the way around to the main doors. It's a separate entrance that allows bar guests to access the parking garage, so that they don't have to fill up the spaces that are reserved for the hotel guests."

Willy glanced over at the entrance, then at the opening to the bar. It was mostly empty at this time of the day, but he still hesitated.

His fingers tightened around her arm and he pressed his face close to her ear. "Are you messing with me?"

Ava winced away, wondering where Felix was. He'd gone to the stairwells that opened to the outside.

That's when she spotted movement. Dear heaven, Felix was literally jumping from one landing of the stairway to the next. The idiot thought he could fly!

Hoping that Willy hadn't noticed, she pulled his attention back to her. "Willy, would you want to go through the front door? I thought you wanted to get the hell out of here? All I want is to be sure Grant is safe. But if you want–"

"Shut up, bitch!" he snapped into her ear, spraying her with spittle. He looked around, obviously trying to determine if she was lying to him. In the end, he nodded, then jerked his chin towards the bar exit. "Fine. We'll go through the parking garage. I'm parked on the first floor anyway." He tightened his grip on her upper arm. "But one wrong move and I call my men and they'll slice your pretty boyfriend's skin into appetizers!"

Ava gasped, horrified, as Willy chuckled.

"You're a sick bastard," she hissed in a low, furious voice.

"So I've heard," he snickered, pushing her towards the doorway.

Ava saw Pierce walking towards the bar. Jenna was positioned by the front door, speaking with one of the cleaning crew. It took another ten steps before she saw Felix out of the corner of her eye. Her brother was now hanging from the railings with his feet holding him in place. No wonder he'd removed his tie, she thought inanely.

"Try anything stupid, and your boyfriend will suffer," he sneered as he opened the door to the outside.

Several things happened at once. First, Pierce spun around in what could only be called the most elaborate dance move she'd ever seen, grabbing her wrist and pulling her out of a thoroughly surprised Willy's grasp. Willy was immediately distracted, so he didn't see Felix above them, who grabbed Willy by the shoulders. There was only a squeak as Willy was tossed from the first floor doorway onto the sidewalk outside. Ava watched in astonishment as Jenna stomped on Willy's hand as he tried to pull a pistol from his jacket. Her spiked heel stabbed through Willy's palm, pinning him in place. Willy screeched in pained panic. But before Willy could more than yell in protest, Felix did a back flip off the railing to land right beside Willy's head. Felix snatched the pistol and aimed it at Willy's face.

Amidst the chaos, Grant pulled up to the curb, got out of the vehicle, and looked around. "What the hell is going on?" He walked over to where Willy was lying on the ground. "Willy, I thought Milo requested your presence in his office?"

Another voice called out. "No problem," the voice interrupted. Milo stepped out of a limousine, buttoning his suit jacket. "When my subordinate didn't arrive within the requested time frame, I had my men find him." Milo walked over to Willy, who was still on the ground, with Felix still standing over him with the pistol, although Jenna had backed up. Milo bent down, looking at Willy's terrified features. "Willy, what have you done?" he asked softly.

"Do you know this man?" Felix demanded.

Milo stood up and shook his head with obvious disappointment. "Yes. He is an employee of mine."

Felix looked around, assessing the situation with rapid speed. He flipped the pistol around with a flair that would have impressed James Bond, offering the grip to Milo. "I trust you will take better care of your employees going forward?"

Mila took the weapon and pocketed it. "It would be my pleasure." He snapped his fingers and two men stepped out of the limo. They advanced on Willy, who screamed in terror at the sight of them. They hoisted him up by the arms and hauled him off to the limo.

Milo turned back to Felix, eying him up and down. "You could have a very lucrative career with me."

Felix chuckled. "I prefer designing buildings. But thank you for the lovely offer." He even winked playfully at Milo who, thankfully, chuckled and turned to leave. "Have a nice day."

Ava rushed over to Grant, throwing herself into his arms. "You're safe!" she gasped, burying her face against his chest. Grant lifted her into his arms, her bare feet dangling a foot off the ground as he held her securely in his arms. "You are too," he whispered. "Willy won't ever bother you again."

She didn't lift her face away from the protection of his chest. "I know that." She looked over at the departing vehicle, then up at Grant. "What did you say to that other man? What's the hold you have over Willy?"

Grant pulled back, setting Ava down as he looked into her eyes. "It doesn't matter anymore. Willy won't bother you ever again." He paused, looking at her sternly. "I thought I told you to stay in the hotel room," he rasped, green eyes filled with concern as he pushed the dark hair out of her eyes. "What happened, Ava?"

"I don't know the name of that guy," she babbled, waving a hand negligently over her shoulder. "Felix stopped Willy from hauling me away and that other guy stopped Felix from shooting Willy."

Grant still didn't understand. So he looked at the threesome standing on the sidewalk, lifting an eyebrow in question.

Pierce chuckled, his arms folded over his chest as he explained, "I believe we have you to thank for Mr. Zanika's departure without my sister?"

Grant's only response was a tightening of his jaw.

Pierce shrugged. "I don't care how, I'm just relieved that Ava is safe."

Grant didn't bother to explain that Willy might not be long for this world. And if Benny Matero didn't take proper care of his employee, then Grant would do the honors for him. He looked over Ava's head at her brothers and corrected his assumption. Felix, with the Navy SEAL trained muscles, might get to Willy before Grant could. Grant kissed the top of Ava's head, rubbing her back comfortingly. "Are you okay, love?" he asked softly, gazing down at the woman who he'd loved for so long.

"Yes," she whispered. "I was so worried!" Ava pulled back and punched him in the arm.

Grant grunted even though her jab hadn't actually hurt. "What was that for?"

"For putting yourself in danger!" she explained, angrily wiping a tear from her cheek. "I was terrified for you! And you just...just...!" She lost the battle and burst into tears, burying her face against his chest again.

Grant still wasn't sure what was going on, so he looked at the three others still standing on the sidewalk. Felix walked over and whispered in his ear, "If you hurt her again, I'll make sure that you disappear in a way that no one will ever ask questions." Then he walked back into the building.

Jenna stepped up next and said, "If you hurt my baby sister again, I will destroy your entire business." She also walked into the building, adding a little huff and a glare over her shoulder right before the glass doors closed on her.

Grant turned to the last remaining sibling. Pierce Halliday was taller than his brother by about an inch, but not as muscular. Felix really outdid the muscle thing, in Grant's opinion. And Jenna? Yeah, she could probably do some damage to his business, but nothing he couldn't handle.

Pierce? This man was a very different kind of risk. He didn't issue threats, but danger lurked in his eyes. There was more to the oldest Halliday sibling's gaze. There was contemplation and...dare he say it... understanding?

Ava pulled away, then stepped out of his arms, wiping at her eyes with the back of her hand. "I'm sorry," she whispered. "That was...emotional of me."

Grant looked down at her tear-drenched beauty and groaned, pulling her right back into his arms. "You're not getting away from me this time, Ava." And with that vow, he kissed her, completely ignoring the oldest brother as he kissed the only woman he'd ever loved. The only woman he could ever love!

Pulling away from her, he sighed and tucked her against his side as he remembered Pierce. Sure enough, he was still glaring at them.

"You're not going to hurt her again." It wasn't a question. It was a statement. Pierce didn't bother to wait for an answer. He simply nodded his approval, then turned and headed for the doors. "I'll get Jenna to reserve the main ballroom for next month."

Grant stared after the man, wondering what he meant. A ballroom... for a wedding? The main ballroom? No, Ava wouldn't want a large wedding. He suspected that she'd prefer a smaller wedding. Maybe in that garden courtyard off to the side, near the pool.

Ava wiped her tears away and told herself to pull away from Grant. But at the moment, he felt too wonderful. Grant was alive! Ava was safe! Her man hadn't been killed by doing whatever he'd done earlier today! There hadn't been a knife anywhere near his ribs. He hadn't been tied up and threatened. That had all been a lie by Willy, the bastard!

"Are you okay?" Grant asked quietly.

"Yes," she whispered. But was she?

"Are you sure?"

She laughed, wondering when the man had become a mind reader. "I'm wrinkling your shirt," she muttered.

"Don't worry about my shirt," he growled. "I like having you hold me like this. And I like you showing me how much I mean to you."

He took her hands and led her to his car. "I think it's time for us to talk," he said, opening the passenger door so that she could get in.

Ava slipped into the soft leather seat and watched as he came around to the driver's side. It occurred to her that she still didn't have her shoes, her cell phone was still up in the abandoned hotel room, and she didn't have even her purse. She was a mess, her mascara was probably streaked down her face and…and none of that mattered, because Grant was safe!

So, she snuggled down into the soft leather of the passenger seat and tried to calm her nerves.

"Where are we going?" she asked as he took the exit towards one of the higher end neighborhoods in Seattle.

"I want to show you something. I need your opinion about an important issue."

He continued to drive, heading down a tree lined street. This neighborhood was filled with large, beautiful houses, each different in style, but each one lovely and eye-catching. She'd looked in this area when looking for her house, but they'd been too large for just her. She'd wanted something cozier.

"Why are we here?" she asked, when he pulled into a house that was huge, with several turrets, a bay window off to the left side, and a huge front yard filled with trees.

"I'm considering buying this house," he told her as he parked the car. He stepped out and came around, meeting her as she stood beside the Lexus. "I won't buy it if you don't like it."

She blinked, pulling her gaze away from the Victorian style house. "What do you mean? If it's your house, you don't need my approval."

He turned, facing her as he took her hands. "I love you, Ava. I don't think I've ever stopped loving you."

She pulled back, trying to pull her hands away. "You don't!"

"I do," he countered, moving closer and trapping her against the vehicle. "And no, I won't let you get away from me this time. I know you love me too."

She gasped, her hands pressing to his shoulders. Not hard, but enough to stop him from coming closer. "What do you mean 'this time'?"

His eyes moved over her features, but he didn't seem angry with her. Still, his words captured her attention. "Eight years ago, you rejected me."

Instant anger boiled up inside of her and she shoved him away. "No! That's not what happened, Grant! You walked away from me! *You* left *me*!"

Grant fisted his hands on his hips, matching her glare with his own. "I didn't leave you, Ava. I asked you to come with me."

She shook her head, memories of their last fight coming back to her. "I couldn't come with you! I had a business to help build!"

He sighed, rubbing a hand over the back of his neck. His glare softened to understanding and he moved closer to her again, but didn't reach for her. "I know that now. But eight years ago, I was furious with you. I thought you'd rejected me. That you didn't love me." He moved even closer, whispering in her ear. "Now I know that you do love me."

Ava stared at his tie, unable to look him in the eye now. But she had to be honest with him. "I loved you eight years ago, Grant."

His hands slid around her waist. "Why didn't you come with me?"

She sniffed and looked away. She stayed silent for a long time. Shame filled her throat, trapping the words. But Grant deserved the truth. It had been eight long years of avoiding that truth. It was time. "Because I was afraid."

There was a long moment of tense silence while both of them processed what she'd just said. Finally, Grant asked, "Afraid of what?" His voice was low and husky, but she could hear the compassion in his tone.

She bit her lip, fighting back tears. And the fear that had never left her psyche. "Afraid that, if I followed you, if I trusted you, that you'd leave me."

Grant's expression softened. "Your father left you."

She took a deep breath, steeled herself, and looked up at him. "My mother died. Pierce went off to college. Felix joined the Navy. Then my father walked out on us." She blinked, remembering the terror of those long, lonely nights. "Jenna and I didn't know what we would eat. We didn't know how we would survive." She sighed, leaning her forehead against his chest. "We were all terrified, Grant. Jenna and I hid our fear from each other, both of us trying to pretend that we weren't scared out of our minds." She paused, squeezing her eyes shut, as if she could banish the painful memories. Finally, she opened her eyes and met his gaze. "But we made it. We figured out how to get people to stay at the hotel. We figured out how to spruce things up to make the rooms more inviting." She pulled out of his arms, stepping away from him. She wrapped her arms around herself before turning back to him. "We were just starting to build a reputation for our tiny hotel when you came into my life." She smiled up at him. "You were so handsome and amazing. You had so much confidence. I wanted to be just like you."

"I didn't know your brothers had just left you, Ava. I'm sorry."

She shrugged. "It doesn't matter now. Pierce came back from Harvard and took over the business side of things. He was brilliant. And Felix..." she chuckled, shaking her head. "He brought his platoon of SEALs back for long weekends. They'd build new cabins and I'd decorate them. They'd goof off in the lake after working all day and Jenna would feed them beer and burgers. They enjoyed the free holiday and we were able to book more customers."

"The SEALs were the ones who built those themed cabins?"

She gave him a teary smile, nodding even though her eyes were filling with tears again. "Yeah. The first one they built was just a solid cabin in the woods. But every time they came back, they had wilder plans ready. I figured they just wanted to challenge themselves by building the most bizarre cabin and make it stronger than what they'd built before. It was the fifth or sixth visit when they decided to build the treetop cabins with the zip lines and wooden access bridges." She sighed and turned, gazing at the beautiful house. "Those cabins were... are...the biggest hits."

"They are still booked up year round, aren't they?"

She laughed, nodding her head as she squinted into the late afternoon sunshine, wiping away the tears. "Yeah. They are impressive buildings, even years later."

There was another long silence. Finally, he asked, "Are you going to admit that you love me?"

She looked up at him. "I do love you." Ava even managed a lopsided grin.

"But you're afraid that I'll leave you again."

She hesitated, but finally nodded. "Yes."

Grant moved closer, pulling her into his arms again. For a long time, they stood there, just holding each other. Finally, he pulled back and pointed to the house. "Let's go inside and I'll show you around."

Ava didn't want to go inside. She wanted to run away.

Grant must have sensed her fears because he took her hands, lifting them up to kiss her knuckles. "I love you, Ava. I'm not going anywhere without you."

She remembered him saying that before. Could she believe him? She loved him so much. What if he left her? Everyone left her!

"Come with me," he ordered, leading her by the hand up the charming walkway to the front door.

"I don't want to go into your house, Grant," she told him.

"It's not my house. It's our house." He used a key to open the door, then added over his shoulder, "As long as you like it, that is."

Ava already adored the house. She just...well, what *was* her issue? He'd said that he loved her. She loved him. He'd bought a house here in Seattle!

"It's..." she didn't have time to finish the statement because he made a beeline for the stairs. "Where are we going?"

"Upstairs." He led her down a long, brightly lit hallway to the owner's suite. It was a massive room with high ceilings and space for a sitting room. There were several doors, which she assumed led to walk in closets and the bathroom, but he went through one of them and stopped in a smaller space. Smaller, but still larger than the bedrooms in her house.

"What's this for?" she asked, looking out through the large windows, down into the enormous backyard.

"I think this would be perfect for a nursery."

Ava's head swiveled around and she stared at him. "Nursery?" she whispered, and an ache she hadn't experienced before, deep down in the pit of her stomach, burst into life. "A...baby?"

"Yes," he answered, his voice gruff. "I want to have children with you, Ava. I don't just want to marry you, I want to build a life with you." He stepped closer. "I know that you feel as if everyone abandoned you. And you probably add me into that category because you feel that I left you too. But I didn't." When she lifted a dark eyebrow at him, he chuckled. "Okay, I did. But only because I didn't think that you loved me. Now, I know better. And I won't let either of us walk away again." He smiled and held out a hand to her. "Ava, we've both been waiting for this moment for so long. For us to work things out. Am I right?"

She couldn't deny it, but the lump in her throat wouldn't let her speak so she took his hand and squeezed.

"Let's do it right this time. Let's talk to each other. No more assumptions. I love you. You love me. We are great together. Why not make this permanent?"

Ava shivered and he wrapped his arms around her, protecting her and assuring her that he was there for her. This, she thought in contentment as she leaned her head against his chest. This was what she'd always craved.

"Okay," she whispered.

Grant pulled back, looking into her eyes. "Okay?"

She laughed, shakily. "Yeah," she whispered, "Okay!"

"Damn I love you, Ava!" he growled, kissing her before she could say the words back to him.

Epilogue

"Oh Ava!" Jenna whispered, watching breathlessly as Ava stepped out of the small room where she'd pulled on her wedding dress. "You're stunning!"

Ava smiled, happier than she'd ever thought possible. "I feel stunning," she whispered back to her sister.

Jenna laughed, then wiped a small tear away. "You're going to wow Grant when he sees you!"

Ava bounced happily. "I certainly hope so!"

Jenna glanced at the clock, then sighed. "It's time," she said, taking Ava's hands in hers. "Are you absolutely sure about this? He hurt you before, Ava. Are you sure that he won't hurt you again?"

Ava's happiness swelled inside of her, causing her to laugh out loud. She hadn't smiled or laughed so much in years. Until Grant came back into her life, her life had been one cautious step after another. But now, it felt as if she were dancing into the sunshine again.

"He won't hurt me, Jenna," Ava replied with absolute confidence. "He'll be by my side, no matter what happens. We're going to have babies and be together forever."

Jenna's smile tightened. A month ago, Ava would have assumed that she'd said or done something her older sister disapproved of. But now that Grant was back in her life, Ava didn't care. She was just too damn happy!

"Let's go," Jenna replied, turning to the small table where bouquets of pink and white roses lay, their stems wrapped in satin ribbons. "You don't want to be late to your own wedding!"

Ava laughed again as she followed her sister. As they reached the back of the tiny courtyard, Jenna handed her the bouquet and Ava took in a slow, deep breath. This was it. This was the moment! She would step through those double doors and commit her life and her love to one man. She'd never been brave enough to think about the future before. Her life had taught her that the people around her were only there for a short period of time.

But not Grant. He would be with her forever!

The music changed and Ava's heart thudded. This was it. Jenna stepped forward and Ava could see the tension in her sister's shoulders. But it no longer bothered her.

Jenna was just about to step through the doors, but abruptly, she turned back. Ava opened her mouth to ask what was wrong as Jenna threw her arms around Ava. "I love you!" she whispered, then pulled back, smoothed a hand down over her pink dress, then walked down the aisle.

Ava was so startled by her sister's hug that she almost missed her cue.

Finally, she stepped out to the small, flower-filled courtyard, her eyes lifting to find...Grant! She hadn't thought that her heart could swell any more, but seeing him standing at the front of the courtyard by the waterfall made her feel as if she might float away with happiness. He was there! Grant was waiting for her!

Grant watched as Ava came toward him. She was so damned beautiful and all he wanted to do was take her hand and pull her into his arms. Wedding, he reminded himself. He had to get through the wedding. This was his woman, he thought. He knew that he'd been waiting for this moment for eight, long years.

"Ava!" he whispered as he took her hand in his. She beamed up at him and he knew that his world had changed forever.

Fifteen minutes later, he heard the words, "I now pronounce you husband and wife." Grant didn't wait for the minister to give him permission to kiss Ava. He lowered his head, pulling her into his arms as he kissed her, vowing with that kiss that he would love her forever!

A message from Elizabeth:

The beginning of a series is always a special time for me. I live with these characters in my mind for months, editing, tweaking, laughing and enjoying each of their personalities. I hope that this book connected you to Ava's personality as deeply.

*If you didn't read "The Beginning", a free prologue for this whole series, check on my website (*https://elizabethlennox.com/halliday-hotel-prologue/ *) to read the story. It's not necessary for any of the books – but just a bit of a background on each of the upcoming characters.*

As always, your feedback is wonderful! If you wouldn't mind, could you leave a review? Got back to your favorite retailer to the book page – and I thank you!

As usual, if you don't want to leave feedback in a public forum, feel free to e-mail me directly at elizabeth@elizabethlennox.com. I answer all e-mails personally, although it sometimes takes me a while. Please don't be offended if I don't respond immediately. I tend to lose myself in writing stories and have a hard time pulling my head out of the book.

Elizabeth

Keep scrolling for a sneak peek at "Felix"- the third book in the Halliday Hotels. Felix is troubled by his past missions with the SEAL teams, but he meets a lovely woman, Giselle, and together, they are able to overcome and flourish!

Excerpt from "Felix"
Release date: June 16, 2023

"I will not be used again."

As soon as she said that last word, she knew she'd messed up. Sure enough, his eyes narrowed and Giselle's gaze returned to his shoulders. Goodness, he was so obviously a warrior! She knew he'd been a Navy SEAL. But she'd never seen a man who could morph so quickly from hot-guy to warrior-guy.

"Who hurt you, Giselle?" he demanded, his voice now low and grumbly. She squirmed, trying to hide how turned on she was at this he-man display. As a modern woman, she shouldn't become excited when a man displayed such behavior. But there was something so basic, so shockingly hot about a man who was ready to defend her.

"He's in the past, Felix," she assured him gently, watching as he leaned back against the leather cushion of the bench. The anger was still there, but the fury was merely banked.

"Who was he?"

She shook her head. "I've moved on." She tapped her book. "I have a list of things that I have decided I need to change about myself in order to become a better girlfriend."

There was another long pause and Giselle suspected that he was debating whether to insist on information about the man who had hurt her. Thankfully, he let it go. For now.

"Let me see it," he demanded.

"No," she replied tartly. "It's *my* list."

He flashed a grin at her defiance and Giselle felt a warm, melting sensation inside of herself.

"How am I supposed to help you with the list if I don't know what's on it?" he countered.

Giselle considered his point for a long moment, unaware of her pursed lips and the impact her expression of concentration had on him.

When her chocolate eyes returned to him, she beamed like she'd just solved world hunger. "I'll tell you what the items are, one at a time. Once you've helped me with one, then I'll tell you the next."

Immediately, he shook his head. "You came to me because you think I'm an expert, correct?"

She bit her lip, then shook her head. "No, I came to you because I don't think you'll let me get away with anything. You seem like the kind who won't let me back slide into my previous habits."

He tilted his head slightly, acknowledging her statement. "Fair enough. You're correct in that assumption." She relaxed, but her relief was short lived. "However, you might think certain items on your list are more important. As a man, I can prioritize the action items from a male viewpoint. So, I need to see the whole list before we start."

Giselle hadn't thought of that, and had to agree that his comment made sense. "Yes, you're right." She considered his argument for another moment, then nodded slowly. "You're absolutely right." She flipped through the pages of her book again and another list fell out. "Darn it," she muttered, then reached out to pick it up. But Felix was faster.

She eyed his long fingers as he read, conjuring up the images from her dream the previous night. Goodness, his fingers were extremely nice. Too nice for a man who worked with his hands. Did he have calluses? She shivered, wondering what it would be like to feel those hard, unforgiving hands on her skin, to know what it was like to...!

Giselle's mind blanked when she realized he was watching her. Were her cheeks as red as they felt? She certainly hoped not! And please please please, don't let him be the kind who could discern her thoughts simply by looking at her expression!

Forcing her thoughts to more...innocent images, she looked back at Felix with what she hoped was a placid expression.

Felix watched her for another long moment, his eyes assessing. But when she merely smiled calmly back at him, he gave up and looked over the list. One of those dark, enticing eyebrows lifted in question. "You made a list of the things you need to clean?"

She blinked at him with confusion. "Of course. Don't you?" She snatched the list out of his hand, glaring at the words.

He chuckled and Giselle had to admit that she enjoyed the sound. "No. I don't clean. I have a housekeeper who keeps my place nice and tidy."

She rolled her eyes as she stuffed the list back into her book. "Well, some of us don't have that luxury. So a list keeps me on track."

She shuffled through the pages to find the correct list and pulled it out, stared at it and...! "Just a moment," she whispered, hoping that her face didn't look as heated as it felt. She put the list on the edge of the table, tearing the last item off and handing him the rest of it.

Made in United States
North Haven, CT
28 February 2024